MW01122755

Normal Madness,
Murder and Mayhem

Normal Madness, Murder and Mayhem

J. Edward Lynch, Ph.D.

To order additional copies of this book, contact:
Xlibris Corporation
1-888-795-4274
www.Xlibris.com
Orders@Xlibris.com
40581

CONTENTS

Hospital People and Some Others

Other Thoughts & Things

Fantasy & Dreams

The Wastebasket Series

The Spiritual

Dedication . . .

This book is dedicated to Barbara Lynch, PhD for her true devotion and concern for me. She said once that she tries to do what will invite people to think best of her in every situation. She does not fail at this. She went to university and got A's in Math and Science and English and Social Studies without attending classes-she is that brilliant. She makes one feel that they are their best self and free. She is a nationally known beader, creator of a Family Therapy program at the graduate level, an author, a mother of nine children, and most important to me, my wife.

Acknowledgements . . .

I want to acknowledge an accident that occurred at Esalen in California. I had a free weekend and no plans yet I thought why not attend a workshop because you meet people easier that way than at lunch. I perused the offerings and decided to do something radically different for myself and that was to take a creative writing course with Deena Metzger. My first creative writing project was titled, "What Got Me Here?" and my final project was, "A Drive to Carmel . . ." the latter being a stand alone offering and lead off for this book.

Additionally, I was supported unfailingly by Jan Doyle. A teacher, a published photographer and author, and television personality, she read my work and was a big encouragement.

I thank all the people whom I have met over the years for their openness and willingness to share their human stories of pain, desolation, and despair.

I also want to acknowledge Dr. E., Dr. C., Dr. J., and especially Mr. P. who came into my life and changed it for the best. He will be with me until I die.

I do not forget my reader and major help in life, Barbara,

J. Edward Lynch, PhD

A Drive to Carmel

Winding roads and split heads and falling rocks and danger and golf courses and even people. He was insane, or at least heading that way and not wanting to, but life is painful. He loses slowly but surely, as he gains more miles. Will he be crazy before even getting to Carmel? He thought, "Yes, indeed, I will." So he decided to go with the process intimately and in tune with the decompensating. How to do it? He needed to and wanted to know, but there is no one to ask, as he is alone in the car. So on his own and either imagining it or it truly happening, he let go of his birth date and the stories around it. He decided to let it die and he felt a beginning invisibleness in his body. Next, he decided—as if he had the power—to let go of all the life occurrences in the first four years of his life. He decided to unlearn the learning of the ABC's. Erase the existence of 'A,' he laughed. How foolish! I guess I am nuts! He laughed a whole half-mile.

C_rmel, 10 miles said the sign. He gulped and burped and thought, "I am the madman!" He proceeded to eliminate the letter 'B,' then 'C,' and as he did so, he began to feel the concentration and focus of his boy First Grade self, self-consciously making a letter.

_ _rmel, 8 miles to go. "I'm getting there—closer to insanity—and it ain't so bad." After he had eliminated all the letters of the alphabet he could read no sign, but he used the mile numbers to determine how far to get to town. What town, anyway? Next he decided to eradicate walking by going to pre-walking, that is, crawling, but he was so successful in his mind that he almost went off the highway into the Pacific. "Leave that one for later," he chose. Not smelling anything anymore was easy. Tasting, not hard to let go of either. Next he wanted to get rid of hearing, but first one more song on the radio—Ray Charles' "I Can't Stop Loving You." Then it happened. His hearing slowly passed—deaf now. Next the sounds in his head. "This is going to be a little more difficult." He began to weep—"Why do I have to go like this? To go insane, well my cooperation with it gives me some power (at least I think so.)" When the driver had finished eradicating the alphabet from his mind, he couldn't see words and sentences any longer. Pity, words are important. Now he decides, at least he thinks he does, to let go of images—thousands that have given him what he calls his life and memories. He can still drive, although he is beginning to feel a slowly growing loss of control in the movement area as well. Pictures are difficult to let go of. I can recall not wanting to toss old photos. But to begin to throw out pictures in the mind that somehow have grounded one in one's life is horrific. He knows he must cooperate with this increasing disintegration. At what speed is it occurring? He does not know, as he is unable to judge time or even tell time now. He feels a deep dread that fills his belly as if replacing his intestines—no, in fact it **is** replacing his intestines. "Oh, I don't know. Oh, the images—yes, let me ride on their back a last time. What will happen to me when I get to the last one?" More dread. Maybe I should fight this? No, I know it is futile. Images and pictures of my children at all ages—gone! My heart shatters. Images of my wife cut away like pieces of wood. Another crushing blow! My mom and dad—I can't see them anymore. I understand blindness in a new way. What will be my last image? Please, God, a good one! Or should it be bad?—easier to let go of a bad one. Who will be the last person I see before I die? I hope it is my loyal, dedicated, caring, loving wife. But no. I'm here on the West Coast and she is elsewhere. I wish, no I don't, she could be with me now. She would see my courage in this but feel me tenderly slipping away. If my crazy lunatic mind can gift me, let my wife be my last image, but too don't let her suffer me long. A visible air is coming between me and the world now. How strange. You are the one who takes over and I can't even cooperate, as now I have no mind. I can see more what my eye sees. I see flowers along the road but I see them without names. I pull the car over and stop it and I get out and look at the mountains. I see them before they were identified for me. It is amazing. That visible air gives me a last chance to see what my eye sees. Now my mind is beginning to leave me, taking its remaining contents. Just one second before I go, I see and hear and smell and taste and touch and I feel blessed. I see God coming. I don't know how long my body will go on, but my mind is gone. I will continue in some way long after . . . . I'm gone . . .

J. Edward Lynch, PhD

Dr. Joe Series

The Madness . . .

Green tentacles coming out like pink sleigh bells, breathing water into my skull thru my ears, eyes that sound like potatoes hitting the ground, merchants running to hide me from their fierce and walking dollhouses. Mish, mash, mush soup beds of nails, scalpels melting into spongy spoons. Spectacles for my feet seeing thru my heels the sky in topsy turvey tree turning tunnels, tinted daybreaks of colorless jade. Winding roads of madness excreting a slew of hate and disgust. Ugh, meow, woof, bleep, peep my toes running away with the sounds. Running in squares from bedside to bedside making a mark on the floor kneeling down in a pigsty of thoughts and swill full of my personality and misgivings. Unending rhythmic skating in a cup full of snow for some blind young fellow. Collars of paste and pearl and pails of putrefied food meeting a boy who wets his pants in pain not too reliving. Circles gone square like and squares are triangles and pentagons are buildings of desire. Crowed streets of meat and mess and bodies passing air and lay in their heads aren't what passes in mine. Tables flying with waterpicks with human remains inside. Declining visions of mute rubber cars. Hands of diamonds and steel and openings/closings of shoe shops and pedicures and people with big feet coming out their noses. Magazines of feathers and glasses of wood flow into an empty river, dead, dying and alive too. Thrashing about the bed, the body sleeps tight and doesn't participate in the insanity of it all. No awareness of plums to see thru in the nose, no care to know anything but occasionally see out into a regular room a split second of time and back to my pictures of all and everything, and sometimes. God comes and He stands with me asking me to save the world in His honor and telling me I'm his son born after Jesus, the second son of God like me my son. You must enter into the world as second born to me and a woman and we will make you one of them and you will discover your godliness in time. First you must understand your mind and sort out the contents and meanings before you can go be born. You will be born in a small town to a catholic couple who are in pain and suffering since from their own childhoods. They will not know who you really are. They will be people of average intelligence, average jobs and mostly troubled inside themselves. They will not give you much love but it is not their weakness, as they never received it. So don't hold them accountable for an empty vessel. You will not know love well either until you discover your diverse nature and then you can begin to perform miracles of healing. I like it when God talks to me, as everything seems clear and correct. When God goes away my mind is jumbled again but on this visit I think he gave me a way out. The kaleidoscopic mind actions have meaning! Circles gone square makes perfect sense to me now! Green tentacles coming out like pink sleigh bells makes so much sense now and tinted daybreaks of colorless jade is obvious too. I feel at peace with this new knowledge and I will share it with others but if only they understand my language. I don't know how I got into this foreign country but I think I've adjusted to the culture. Here comes a black man, I will try to again to talk with him. : "Ge lr mm ha be n su ca po." No, he does not seem to understand me. I'll let him hold my slippers again to see if he can talk to me thru the silk or the souls. No, I do not understand a word he is saying either. He sounds like a nice man. I'll tell him I am the second son of god-right now!" Lo xx stl aa liku tu ze." He doesn't understand and I think I am going crazy again this is not my choice! The devil is coming over me now I can't help it! Can't you see me in here with all this horror? I want out of me out of me!! Urghh!! My skin is crawling and now I see bugs flying in my eyes, and my blood I feel moving in my veins 10 miles per hour. Blue books of crepe suzettes, pages of feathers again, bones of candy striped nurse's aids, black people screaming with wide open hands, smells turning purple in my elbows, accordions flashing their genitals . . . .

Doctor Joe . . .

The doctor, tired now from so much time in his inner prison of pudding mind, creative yet but bland in a sick way. Ruminating thoughts of flying to and fro, inside where no one reaches him, he still is a doctor and he feels his heart pounding and slowing down as if in time with some dying heartbeat. Maybe he is a dying blood moving slowly through his veins. The doctor identifies himself as the drops of blood flowing along in his body through the aorta and down other veins like a rollercoaster in slow motion. A bloodcoaster, flowing along with him attached. I am my blood moving, my moving blood. I' m blue, slow, and constantly on the same route. Now up to the brain and surely to go down again on a familiar traveled path. When they look at me they think I am in my eyes, but I am all over inside at different times. Sometimes when they draw my blood I almost go out with the blood. Don't they know they have some of my essence? They are partializing me into more and more fragments. I turn red out there—red rage royale. Sometimes when my oxygen gets turned into me I get frightened—will there be enough room in my system? My slippers keep me soft and warm and blue curried cool. When I eat, I feel myself turning into blood and cells and growth and this is why I am totally crazy. Tune yourself into this—this primitive pre-self monstrous and small substance. I am consumed with every movement my body makes, even the most subtle eyebrow move. I attend to all of me all the time and I am constantly overwhelmed and drowning in a body of whirlpool quagmire desolation. Look at me—you don't see this, do you? You see a normal body, but with some bizarre behaviors and sound-making. You test me and CBC me and don't know that I am in my liquids and movements and out of my mind. Look into my mind if you choose—no one home—get it? Your science can't help me cause you look in the wrong places. Be absolutely absurd and find me!

The Doctor, again . . .

Brown buckets of bloody bleak meaning. Swirling sexual pictures meeting a counterforce of pure hellish images in the head. Which brain collapsed? Probably the reptilian broke into the mind instead of staying dormant and civilized. He is pre historic now, civilization failed in his mind. It did not take hold, something else did, something with more power and presence. The Doctor watched his demise from a distance inside himself, when the mind's movies overcame his ability to resist them; he collapsed into a raging, crying, beast. Paranoia pushed in and liked what it saw and decided to take up residence. The doctor might flail against the images but without a successful outcome. He will need to learn to live with the craziness as it worsens and his touch with reality becomes more brittle and tender. In time, maybe some kind of new medicine will help, but for now only sedation exists and that only for his movements not for the internal anguish filled pictures. No, whoever that photographer is will go untouched. He works for his own conscience and needs. Perhaps the Demon internalized? Why not call it so? Is an exorcism in order? Out of control behavior, frightening and rapid, intensifying and diss-appearing only to spontaneously flash back again. It has its own mind in the doctor's mind. The mind within the mind within the mind rules now. Poor doctor, why him? Well, remember some of his history, so what better place for him to go to, though painful, but into the deep abyss. His brother went to hell because of alcohol and lack of intelligence. A mind contraction/expansion waiting to happen and nobody cares.

The Doctor . . . #2

The doctor, again, insane, mad, a lunatic. His father was a shoemaker from Italy who had sexually consumed himself in an attempt to hide from his sexuality. Woman after woman, Don Juanesquely, he would seek them out for relief from his deep painful fear/knowledge of his difference. Finally, and in a fateful way, he tried a man. Yes, he was drunk so it wasn't really his choice, fault, decision, but a strange relief pervaded his whole body, mind, and spirit. Home, he said to himself, finally home. What would happen if he were sober and alert and fucking? He wondered what would happen. He could only be drunk he thought to do this formally called horrible deed. His son, Joe, looked at him with crazy eyes-he knew that to be true. But the father never held him and rarely talked to him-too busy repairing shoes and chasing women that brought them into his little shop. His wife waited a while in the marriage but anyone would leave this man-now beyond the normal mistress activities and into the town's women. So try a man but sober this time. And indeed he did with great anxiety and joy and fulfillment too. He saw new images in his head of twisting bodies into shapes he could not imagine. Joe, his son, found him in one of his fucking encounters with two men and this boy—very intelligent-seemed to dismember his soul and heart with the knife of his own eyes. Joe, falling inside into a frightening, screaming, dead hole disappeared linked to visual images into his unconscious mind-but not forever just for now to make the next footstep out of the backroom of the shop. The street, white and beige, somehow blackened now thru damaged eyes and spirit. What can Joe make, do, or think of this in his little heart? My daddy is crazy and naked and making animal sounds bizarre. Joe, who later became a doctor, would go back to the shop only when his father was seen on the doorstep having a smoke—then it was safe to know he would not see the devil scene-or was it? Every now and then Joe's mind would light up like the evening sky filled with stars attached to words and phrases that would sail across his mind line disconnecting from any solid surface creating a floating feeling all over such that his mind seemed elsewhere not in his head. What beautiful motions they would have. As an adult, now a doctor, Joe lost himself in his floating mind and one day did not come back. He sat down on one of the floating word phrases and slowly drifted away.

The Doctor's Tilde of View

Why don't they understand me? I'm talking, ain't I? Don't they understand my language? I am a doctor in a neurological complex on the outskirts of town, but I am in residence as a crazy person. I had a complete flyout in my mind. I had gaping holes in my inner head, unending flat surfaces, words zipping around on the backs of water, images drowning in marshmallows, my feelings acting like pistons in an engine, my thoughts evaporating into white lights that blinked like eyelids and no one was there. I'm a shoemaker surgeon crazy man locked up in here and there is a chasm between me and the world filled with whirlwinds of visible air. I'm crazy. I can't even put on my own shoes, I'm Italian and my daddy was a shoemaker, a cobbler, a queer, and he tried to make me into him but I was intelligent and became a doctor and my intelligence, my father, and myself have destroyed me. I'm odd, now don't you think? Reach into my mind and get lost with me. The colors of DO RE MI and the sounds of the touching hands drive me crazy. I think I'm sinking now more—why don't I die? I heard some jump out the windows here, my windows, like my mind, has bars—no one out and no one in. No one was there when I died the first time. And where is Ed? I think my name is Yahweh.

Dr. Joe, and Jesuses . . .

In a sick, isolated, island way, where you feel the limits of freedom, he could rove around inside. Joe had been here for four years now and not much had changed in the place or in him. Still crazy inside with minimal thoughts and cohesions, he felt tired of it but did he really know? Charming and charismatic halucinations of Jesus and others kept him occasionally amused. This new development doctors did not know about anyway. One time he saw three Jesuses is and they were arguing about who had been sacrificed on the cross as only one could claim it to be true. Jesus #1 decided to claim the youth of Christ, Jesus #2 to claim the middle years and Jesus #3 claimed the last years of the life of Christ. Arguments also occurred around Joseph and Mary. Which one did Jesus love more, which was favored, etcetera. Joseph influenced with his male energy Jesus #1. Jesus #2 claimed the femininity of Mary which gave him access to his homosexual apostles. Jesus #3 became a priest in Nazi Germany. Yes it was confusing to Dr. Joe butit also made sense because he was insane and some things make more sense when you are insane rather than sane. Dr. Joe knew this had been scientifically and artistically proven.

My name is Josephina . . .

"Wow! How lucky! I made it just in time. Could've been late but no just in time". Where was she going? Who could really know without her telling the truth? Words spoken can be lies even to the speaker tho she won't know it but think it the truth. She was crazy and was Dr. Joe in disguise to all. A part of his personality, some might say his 'anima' gone crazy, in a symbolic vagina way—very convoluted. Go west in a teacup full of lhasa apsos mixed with sugar and candied shih tsu puppies all encased in a glass slipper made from a carrot dangling by the road on the end of some donkey strip base of love. Oh, here is the crazy lunatic mind coming again. This time it came out in the form of a woman and her goings on—sad but true. Watch her sentences go along and unfold into lily contadas of waffles filled with barrycleese and Sunday morning expertise-sense who cares-I just took in a breath and can go on—what else matters? Creeping criteria crawling credit countings. She likes the letter "C". In my name Jocephina there is a "C. A "C" makes sounds sometimes softly, and sometimes loudly, but always easy to hear. It can sooth you or disturb you with a cacophony of unending waves, visions of pure sound dropping into goblets of nowhere. "C", she says, and all agree with her in this murky, watery, slime of mindfulness. Swimming in the "Si" of promise in another time given as possibilities to surrender to God. "I like me', he/she says out loud, a sound for the first time.

I Am the Walrus . . .

Walrus madness about words and writing. Well Russ? What wall? Who Russ? What equals unity? 3 in 1—isn't that an oil of some kind? Look how I go off like I'm in analysis crazy everything means something/nothing. Is this the Path? Wow another thought. Look at the terrible writing of an inner less clear slow demise into a madness welcome? I'm ahead of it like I have been with many other things and trends. Is my unconscious leading me and letting me know my future? Exactly what is a walrus symbolically? A Lennon/Beatle thing, I know, but before that? A prehistoric monster to some. Am I simultaneously being pulled into the past and present at the same time,—being in the present. Primitive and destructive—just participate in current and constructive for a while, then be pulled into two opposing directions? Kind of crazy, yet very possible to happen? Who knows what may actually happen. Which pull feels stronger—the past or the future in this present—I write more about now in the past and future than I do about then in the past and future or to come in the past and future. What do I need to do? Let it emerge as it happens? Is this impossible or co-creative? What do I want? What do I want? What do I want to do? What do I want to do with what's left? Partially accept what emerges and create it simultaneously, too. Is that a possibility? Yes, of course—to emerge and create at the same time. Am I wordless vocabularyless or can I do it? Compare consequence of introjects—guilt bad wrong below the line—accept I'm wrong guilty bad above the line makes life easier to manage. Is it a trick or does it come from the heart? A bitter,a better heart. Is change merely being quiet about what one used to say? Is change inhibition of spontaneity? Yes, I think it can be—OH, WELL! What do I mean by that tuff shit or resignation or acceptance. I think resignation is the answer like Mom—What a good son—Family Constellations, here I come. Guilt good bad here I come where am I going and what happened to the walrus?

Let Me Go . . .

Humming, rocking, stomping, raging full of life but life looked upon as the negative side of it. What can I do with these forces inside me I can't control? Live till I die, no? Just like everyone else, right? I did not ask for this wall between me and the world. I did not ask for this body to be mine. What am I to prove or learn or do by being crazy? What about all my years of medical training and practice, what was that for when now I cannot even talk to you or understand you? What is the point of my life as I sit here rocking and as an invisible? Am I to be gawked at by you and watched and prodded? For what reason is this me? Why don't you inject death into me? It is costing thousands of dollars to keep me alive and to be seen this way? Black, bleak visions now creep into my head, extensions of some outer space tentacles wrapping me into some darker blackness of my mind. Entwining me into me into many mes of confusion and fright and despair. Thank you for life but mine ended the day I broke down in my office and worsened since. You have nothing to help me. Go look in and write in your books about me. Present me at Grand Rounds as a puzzle to solve. Talk about me as an object to be known. Go ahead in your futility see what you can conjure up about me. Pity me from the deepest place in your heart, yes, go on and thank you

The Professor is the Madman

Jauntily laughing crazy walking, scoffing all in his head hidden deep in the insane asylum of his own person, he sits to eat. This lovely old professor and madman is quite happy for your information. Swinging seagulls, moving seashells, and lace cornerstones supporting mountains of water all occur in a pink, beige, hue of a cacophony of sounds. What a joy, utter joy to be me he would think. Out of the racetrack or horse trap what was it called the work world—I remember now. Fleeting falcons coursing thru the water and live doves inside an elephant's egg of gray mucous. What student? What kind of measure leads into goat like scampering fertilized fried fruit and beans? Eating, primitive, universal, historical tidy up young man! Foods falling fatuously over the edge of a table like Columbus over the edge of the earth. The world is square like me. Boats falling off an Abigail abyss empty and yet full of time's elements so solid. I am only eating breakfast he thinks but what a hint of things to come. Fruit flies and cabbage cankers and crepe rapers all lined up in a fantasmagorific show of blindness. Categories elude me and ponds fill my mind with muck and mire and a myriad of Moses the blessed ones coming towards me with Jesus in a broken line to the sounds of Waltzing Matilda-what a great song! Finish my eggs with a liquid paint of azure kind, plotting my next infitesimal move-mind or body? Plan? I have no control over emanating egrets walking over the swamp of my mind. What's next? See me falling fast while not moving an inch—here I go fast and not twitching a tad. Shimmy up the table leg into where food is hidden from the monsters in their white coats and cheeses, perhaps a round ball to they go. They can't see me at all. Beatles beetles what? What forever? What wood? Can I see out from here into the world of memory or am I merely a piece of bacon waiting to mate an egg plate. Come together when? For the benefit of whom? Might I be going insane or into health—HELP! No, no don't ask just be merely meagerly man who is as hollow as a bird's bone in a whisper of meanderings. Reach into the existing exit with heart filled grandmotherly coldness-see it for your self, madness of the sweet sense kind where everything floats together and comes apart in a traditional mardi gras of confusion. Madness becomes me. Soon I will die of overdose of mind and lack of it. When I don't know but it will be painless as I walk into that veil and cross that silent sea into some unknown urchin's paradise where my mind will go further than me into Jesus and the depths of afterlife while some of me stays around to haunt you till your own death. Scurry Joseph into your own womb and disconnect lightly with madness of the spiritual kind. Good luck into the way . . .

Crazy You . . .

Maybe I can get out of here on the U of the alphabet! Certainly the U is an important letter-so therefore I will be important too. Question. Should I emphasize the sound of U in a long way like in 'use' or should I make the short sound like in untie. What a decision! I am going with the long sound U. When the nurse comes by I will hold the U in my mind and she will see I have recovered my sanity. Why did I not think of this before? She will see U and set me free-I am sure of it, and U can be seen very easily. I exed out W as it has those awkward tops that would not fit thru. U can stand alone, or with others I have got to be ready to show U how to keep mentally strong. Be ready for when she comes by my door. Oh Dear! I am getting confused, as the U that is in me is getting mixed-up with me! I do not trust U to take me out of here but if I get free can I take U and not me? As she walks by she looks at me, not U, and so I stay till next time-not good for you or me.

Joseph the Resident

Joseph is a resident in the Neurological Complex on the outskirts of town. He is a beautiful man, non-functioning. He was a doctor and, curiously, knew the trade of the shoemaker. I do not know how he put these two together in his daily life but as a surgeon, perhaps the skills were interchangeable. Working with soul is not easy I am thinking. And working with patients is difficult too. His work somehow touched a deep unknowing place in himself that he could not sustain or integrate. What was the final loss of contact with reality, no one knows. No one was there. Joseph now looks beautiful and dismal, bleak and peaceful and has no patients or souls to work with. He walks around all day I am told. I cannot visit him, it is too painful. He talks in gibberish, a language I wish I could learn. He is gone never to return unless someone cures him-maybe a doctor will. I hope Joseph does not kill himself tho he wouldn't know it was him anyway. Maybe he would go someplace interesting like where surgeon shoemakers gather. I think he is Italian-he once built a stonewall-maybe I'll go see him-I'm one of his patients and he worked on my soul too.

Waiting . . .

Waiting for Dr. Joe to emerge from his madness is a futile task. He'll never come out of it-he is too far into it now. It has been three years and a few months. What happened in his office that day in town we'll probably never know. What we have is that Joe was found on the floor screaming at the top of his lungs in a language that no one understood-a gibberish. He had finished with his patients for the day just one half an hour before his breakdown. The doctors and the police too talked to his patients of that day, but they reported nothing unusual about the Dr. Joe. There may have been some sort of harmonic convergence in his mind-too much to bare inside alone. The Dr. Joe had lived alone his whole adult life, sad to say. He was cordial to his patients, but not overly interested in them. He did a good job and remained professional. He had no staff, taking care of billing and office duties himself. His family had disintegrated and not any of his siblings were married or in relationships of any promise. His sister was part owner of the bakery in town and his brother who had a history of psychiatric care lived in a hotel downtown. There was no contact amongst these siblings. They were considered strange and aloof as children, having no friends or companions either. The mother was hardly seen outside the house, hidden almost by the four walls of it. She had come from Italy and didn't bother to learn English. She came on the boat at a very young age, and alone. There were questions about whom she stayed with upon arrival. Some cousin it seemed, but no one knew for sure where he lived or if he was even a cousin. Joe was the oldest and seemingly the brightest of the three. At medical school he kept to himself and did ok-he fell somewhere at the middle of the class—not great and not bad. He lost himself in the books at the time and did not bother much with his peers. Since he returned to town, he still kept to himself after hours. There was some talk of his night-owling in the seedier neighborhoods but that was never proven to be true. He opened his office with little fanfare and grew a practice slowly over time. He did not work excessive hours, as the light would not be on at night. He shopped around town but didn't seem to be noticed when outside his office. He did have a nondescript common kind of face and build. Much like a voyeur who can stand and blend into the surroundings, it was as if Joe couldn't be seen. (He is not a voyeur). If he had any hobbies, it was unknown. Occasionally he would linger in front of the shoemaker's shop but never went in. It is believed that his father was the original cobbler in town and had this shop but he long ago disappeared. Dr. Joe had a gracious smile though someone said it was a pro's smile. His voice had a low quality to it and it sounded gravelly. He had brown eyes that sometimes appeared black in a certain light. When he was taken from his office that day to the neurological complex, he went into violent rages against the police and they put him into a straight jacket and he ripped one piece of material that held his arm in the jacket. He was in a rage powerfully. It took six men to get him into the rubber room where he could be sedated and observed for a few days. He calmed down on the meds and became quite docile though he could lose it some of the time when the meds were wearing off. Dr. Joe would sit in a chair most of the day fiddling with his slippers. Oddly, one day, a pair of silk slippers were found on the doorstep with Dr. Joe's name on the package. It is not known who left them there but the slippers were given to him and—if possible—they seemed to calm him a bit. At times he would become catatonic-unpredictable as to when. At lunch and other meal times when he was able, he ate with slowness, deliberateness, and precision. His eyes, not clear from the medications, moved slowly from side to side at times landing on no particular object. He did not need help to clean himself except if an accident occurred in a catatonic state. To the disbelief of the staff, every night he would kneel down before his bed and talk in gibberish, probably praying. He also had another ritual he repeated before bedtime. He would walk around to the other side of the bed and touch the wall, then return and do it to the other side three times. It appeared as if he were hanging a covering of some kind. His gibberish was repetitive at these times. Then he would get into the bed and drop to sleep immediately.

You Lunatic!!

Screaming, blood curdling screamings. Flailing and thrashing about in the bed all through the night and he sleeps inside unknowing-maybe just a slight glimpse of it all. I can't control it, my body crazy body much like my mind filled with foreign objects that thrash about. Body and mind, what else have I? No control of either one. I want to kill myself but I cannot even think to know how. I am imprisoned in this wreck of a thing. Can anyone see me? I am the star in the solar system one of billions-pick me out!! Flying through each solar system, I change my watch to the current time. My body adjusts to twenty-four hour jet lag without being in an airplane. My stomach holds at the height of vomit spill not quite over the top its puss and boil lanced fluid like soft dinks. My eyes have fallen into my throat. Only to be swallowed whole. My nose smells from inside my body, smells of blood moving and lymphatic juiciness and intestinal drudge and scum of fecal matter. I taste the height of vomit and the cool smooth texture of spleen and bile and the air between all the organs so putrid. My movements designed by a maddened choreographer like a puppet on a metal rope almost like a hanging. Didn't I pray as a sane little boy or was that the beginning of madness? Didn't I experience God or was that the demon in form? The day I drank from sober to drunk to sober? All that Tab? My biophysiological chemical makeup from birth? From the grass eating ancestors? Where did my mind come from? A smudge or a liquid or a gesture? I am falling deeper into this horror, what can I do to help myself? Nothing, nada, no. Split open my femur the vertical way, then my arms and each of my ribs the long way, dissect my skull into chewable vitamins for children and build a bone cane and bone hat for the sun time. Alone? You bet!

On The Way . . .

    The doctor, tired now from so much time in his inner prison of pudding mind, creative, yes, but bland in a sick way. Ruminating thoughts flying to and fro. Inside, where no one reaches him, he is still a doctor and he feels his heart pounding and slowing down as if in tune with some dying heartbeat. Maybe he is dying, blood moving slowly thru his veins. The doctor identifies himself as the drops of blood carried along in his body thru the aorta and down other veins like a rollercoaster in slow motion. A Bloodcoaster, flowing along with him attached. I'm my blood moving along my moving blood. I am blue, slow and constantly on the same route. Now up to the brain and surely to go downward again on a familiar traveled path. When they look at me they think I am in my eyes but I am all over inside at different times. Sometimes when they draw my blood, I almost go out with the blood. Don't they know they have some of my essence? They are partializing me into more and more fragments. I turn red out there—red rage rugula. Sometimes when my oxygen gets turned into me, I get frightened. Will there be enough room in my system? My slippers keep me soft and warm, and blue curried cool. When I eat, I feel myself turning into blood and cells and growth and this is why I am totally crazy. Turn yourself into this-this primitive pure self, monstrous, and small substance. I am consumed with every movement my body makes, even the most subtle eyebrow move. I attend to all of me all of the time and I am constantly overwhelmed, drowning in a body of whirlpool quagmire desolation. Look at me. You don't see this, do you? You see a normal body but with some bizarre behaviors and sound makings. You test me and CBC me and don't know that I am in my liquids and movements and out of my mind. Look into my mind if you choose-no one home—get it!! Your science cannot help me cause you look in the wrong places. Be absolutely absurd and find me!!

I Did It for You . . .

He was a former Catholic priest and now an Episcopal priest, as he " . . . couldn't do without the sex." he reported. He said that he was having difficulty with conflicts in his parish and he had never been able to deal with them. " Why did you become a priest?" I asked him? "I always felt a calling." To my facilitators mind " . . . having a calling" implied that someone with a voice was talking to him and making the call. I wondered to whom this voice might belong. I asked him how many siblings did he have and he said, " One and that his mom and dad were devout Catholics. I thought that they may not practice birth control and asked him if there were any stillbirths or miscarriages, as the devout ones would not tolerate abortions. He reported there were eleven. "Of which type" I asked. "Nine miscarriages and two stillbirths." I thought how painful it must have been for those parents with all the losses. I felt immediately pulled to ask him to pick representatives for all the siblings and he and his sister. He proceeded to do it and I asked him to put them in the order of their soul births. And then I heard, "Name them." When he finished lining them up it was quite an outstanding scene. He looked humbled by it. I said, "Name them" and to my surprise he did it without hesitation even once. "Mary, Sean, Bridget . . ." and the rest with Irish names that came easily to him. He seemed at ease with them. I wondered, because of the deep spiritual feeling, if I was present at a symbolic baptism and that these were the real names of these souls. Spontaneously he said, "If they had all been born I would know how to handle conflict," and we enjoyed the humor and seriousness of the comment I wanted to asked him again why he wanted to become a priest. He said, "They were calling and I did it for them. He filled with tears. I asked him could he bless them and he said he was just thinking the same thing. And he did. I told him on this night he should have them all over for dinner and he agreed but would have to figure out how to get them all around the table. I said to him that they would back him up and be with him in the conflicts from now on and he said, "With this team I can learn a lot." I said "Is this a good place to stop for now? He said, "I think I am just beginning." We stopped.

The Townspeople

Joe's Mom and Dad . . .

Striking, beautiful, and luminous, she walks though being watched by all. Men are intimidated by her looks, women are jealous. What man could keep her forever? Maybe none. She wonders why she has no male friends last too long. Is it her or them? She grows to be a bit interior minded and slightly off, which makes her more attractive. The young shoemaker in training in this little town of Arco, is attracted to her and she to him. She is the most beautiful young woman in town. She floats, sways, and undulates, walking unselfconsciously along. No attempts to draw attention on her part, yet it comes from all over. Her brown bedroom eyes were distracting to all the men around. The young shoemaker asked her father for permission to see her and he was granted permission, as long as an aunt accompanied them whenever wherever they went dating. The aunt, however, more contemporary than many, would leave them and reunite with them at appointed times. The shoemaker was enchanted by the woman and they would find themselves in their native arms. It was under the grapevines, where with frenzied abandon they would try to release and comprehend their biological, primitive intensities. They never could. Now, succinct, pointed, and driven to release, their bodies would stammer and clash and bleed like the animals of the Kalahari, yet want more. The aunt would never ask about the blood on her niece's neck, attributing it to rose thorns and brambles. How sweet she was! Joe's mom fell in love with the shoemaker, though she thought him a bit odd. He was very intelligent, smart, of the world and uneducated. Why shoemaking? He would say, "My father did it and so will I." Settled, then. The young man would talk about America, the faraway land where opportunity abounded and would she go with him there? Could she leave her family, friends, town, and support? For him and with him, Yes! Yes! Yes! They married and she was soon pregnant and she hoped she wouldn't turn nonsexual like some of the village folk said happened to married pregnant women. She felt so much gratitude to and for her husband and his love for her. It made her sparkle more every day. Would she love her children as much as her husband? She thought not, but needed to wait to see. Maybe it is a different kind of love. Like the town's other girls, she had no skills that she developed, but they were all to marry anyway, and the husbands would make the living and support the family. She was intelligent and she knew it. Open-minded, talented, a beautiful voice and she could dance with grace and ease. She wondered if America would help her develop or would it be the same?

A Nurse Attendant . . .

Why do I have to take care of that nut case for this lousy pay I get! He is a fruitcake if I ever saw one! Damn him! Why don't he die! I'm glad no one knows I think this way, I'd get fired for sure. But that stupid ass surgeon cobbler or whatever the hell he was is my worst case. He is a kook for sure! He makes little motions with his hands like a little girl—I could crush them into little bone pieces. He fondled me once when I was helping him into bed-the bastard—tho later that night I dreamed about him. He may be crazy but he is good looking. I have to clean up his shit if he does not make it to the toilet-his shit looks crazy too. What the hell am I doing working here-I hate it!. It pays the best and the most. I get health care coverage but this neurological complex is so odd to work in. I can't go anywhere else especially with my background in nursing being so weak. I'm only an LPN, but most think I m an RN. Fuck them, none the wiser! My last job let me go. They thought I had something to do with the death of some patients. I didn't of course I did. I almost got caught. I gave them an overdose in such a delicate sneaky way that works and I won't tell anyone what it is. I think I'd like to fuck up this Dr. Joe. Something eerie in his eyes tho, crazy bastard makes me think he sees my thoughts and plans. I know it isn't true but it feels weird anyway-I guess I'm a bit paranoid. He is the one I want to overdose the most. I want to watch him get fucked up completely and not even know he was dying probably thinking it was some virus. Well, he wouldn't know, just the doctors will think it a virus. Crazy Joe wouldn't know only I would. What a triumph that would be-then I would stop this dangerous pleasure I have. I wish I could try it on myself and watch till I was dead but I don't want to die with it-I'm not that crazy. I like my work sometimes, for example, when I get the paycheck and I can go out to places I won't tell you where. I live alone in town where, of course, everyone knows everyone's business.

B and D . . .

Two lives intertwined at least part of the time in fantasy and part of the time in reality. Two young prom goers, two lovers, finally joining in togetherness She, radiant, intelligent, and warm, he, creative, surprising, and calm. She left him years ago for someone whom she married and with whom she had children. In her heart of hearts lingered B., in a deep loving, way. He was unsettled at the loss and became somewhat of a drifter finally at one time ending up as a ski instructor out west. Not long after, he decided to enter the helping professions and ended up working with adolescent offenders, why he couldn't figure out. He came to love a certain therapy that powerfully brought him into touch with himself and he learned to share it with others. One day quite by accident, B and D met and the old flame ignited and the feeling arose like a blue light candle. They talked as if twenty—five years had passed like twenty—five minutes. He loved her and she loved him. They both were free and decided to reconnect and did so with love, compassion, and fun. He built her a music room. She cooked, he cooked, and they walked and planted the garden and lived close to the earth together. They grew older in each other's sight and became wise and true.

Bryce . . .

I cannot have children. I am able but I cannot bring children into this world-I can't be a parent. I would flunk and add to the pain of the world and I won't. The group is . . . angry . . . no response, the group is . . . sad . . . no response, the group . . . is out of the room . . . no response. This goes on often and yet I feel deep within me a movement. What can it be? How can it be? It is there and it is in my heart. What does it wish? What am I to discover? Another week and the group is . . . tired . . . no response, the group is . . . avoiding its task . . . and my heart begins to answer its question. How intriguing! I feel this deep maternal love for these people, truly a deep expansive, enduring, love. They are like little children struggling to know themselves and each other and the world and I am like their mother and I feel it in my essence. These heartfelt feelings move throughout my body to my life giving and carrying self, and onto the paths leading to my soul. How profound this movement of my spirit. I can be a mother!! I begin to weep gently the first birthing tears to come. Please . . . a baby for me! My teary, sexual, heart self feels a unification able to hold and endure any pain to come. I want a boy and I want a girl! I long and yearn now like I never could. Grant me my wish for my life has changed and I am ready for the new. Thank you everybody!

Cookie the Cook . . .

Huge! Huge! Huge! Like almost every cook this one was real big. He ate what he cooked-a lot of it too. Like Jesus with the loaves and fishes who fed thousands, Cookie felt as big feeding the whole complex. He wasn't performing a miracle, but he fed over 200 people a day. He had learned to cook at home as his mother was crippled and could not move around much She directed him on how to prepare food for her and for the rest of the family. Cookie liked his work cause he felt nurturing and as if he were doing the most important thing, feeding folks so that they could do what they had to do. He did not talk much, mostly head nods and grunts and other gestures to get his help to do what he wanted. Cookie's favorite dish was the vegetables. He often felt guilty about it but he had liked them a long time before he came to work where some staff referred to the residents as vegetables. The cook would remember the vegetables by associating to the locales. So, for example, Tomatoes Toronto, Boston Beets, California Cauliflower, Rochester Rugula, Carolina Carrots. It helped him he believed. He also named the patients by their physical symptoms and associated them to cars Dyskinesia Dakota, Cadillac Catatonic, Saturn psychophrenia. It was kind of silly but it was his creation. He had been a cook in he army in the last war and had spit and peed into the soup of the lieutenants and captains when one day they made fun of him cause he did not have to go to the front lines. Cookie had been drafted and became permanent barracks orderly until he had his operation, which took care of his problem and then he became cook for his group. So working here was not unlike other conditions he had seen in his life time. Feeding the 'vegetables' vegetables was easy to do. He was fond of one patient in particular though he saw him infrequently. He was called Dr. Joe but it was probably a nickname of some kind. One time he saw Dr. Joe sitting, mumbling and eating and he just seemed like a good guy to Cookie. In fact he thought that Joe looked a little bit like his own father-that was it! He did look like him and it was a father that he loved very much and missed deeply.

D and D . . .

They stood together near the foundation of their home. Exceptional and yet ordinary people, he with jeans and tee shirt a bit cool for the time, but he generated a lot of heat for he was a bull of a man, broad shoulders and strength apparent. She well and firmly figured, long black hair and a gentle laugh. They look at the foundation—perhaps like the foundation of their marriage-solid, supportive and visible. Together they made a son or id or Oedipus as they sometimes called him, and he was. Their love was viewable and made real in their son. Italian, operatic, passionate and human are they. He opens in new ways like a man in touch-not a boy. She opens like a woman, deep, full of pain and despair, and then reaching into her soul and heart to find the stamina and strength to achieve. The foundation is made of cement and one can imagine as they look, their being in a small town in Italy, speaking Italian, and gesturing to each other. Meanwhile, pasta is cooking on the stove and the dinner table awaits. Unawarely duplicating their ancestors in posture and stance, they represent a link to the soul. His heart quivered for some unknown reason, but it did not break. In the quiver, he opened to more love for himself. She asked to be more received. Let me love you and receive me with my/ your full open heart. Relationships are difficult and they had their triumphs and failures together and separately too. No more children they both said but they also could mix a yearning and mourning in a bittersweet velvet way. Growth is inevitable and fifty percent painful-both he and she are warriors having weathered many personal battles before coming to rest in each other's arms and finally at peace and home.

Dee . . .

Such a dreamer, extend more and more, why not? The possibilities are endless aren't they? I believe that I can achieve anything I want to if I put my mind to it. I am not tilting at windmills like Don Quijote, I dream the impossible dream in a realistic way. I am a deeply spiritual man, and I wish God would manifest more in my experience of myself. I would have become a priest if I could be married. What will I do with all that I have? Should I go back to business" No, into agency work? No, in therapy yes but only if I can be creator of something new maybe about couples, perhaps a new method. I think I want to be famous some day like some people I know. But how to do it, I am not sure. Maybe I can just be an ordinary dad to my son and have that be why I am famous. My God if anything ever happened to him I don't know what I would do. His soul is almost palpable to me and I want to guide him in the right way before I have to go. Maybe in being a good father, therapist, and lecturer, the fame will come, but later. We'll see.

Duna . . .

Grounded at fifteen years old? This is surprising. An adult sense of self-assuredness in an adolescent time. Quiet, and confident, intelligent and curious too. Where is the teenager? Oh, there she is in the tee shirt, baggy clothes, and new sneakers. "What?" she says, as I forget to slow down my English till she gets my cadence and rhythm. Spanish is her native language though she also speaks Catalan, and is learning French too. When I look at her I see Ximo and Lydia too, her parents whose influence has been profound. Ximo's eyes or Lydia's, difficult to tell. Whose nose and mouth, is a close call. Duna is studying ten subjects in school, sounds busy, and is doing well. No mistakes in her English speaking. Sentence construction and pronunciation are clear and she asks me if she has a Spanish accent and when I say no, she beams as if in some triumph. Orlando Bloom, Justin Timberlake, well there is the teen again. Her presence—deep and palpable, like a Mother Earth is unusual for her age. Pensive, and though still young, a maturity. What's this!!! Playing on the floor with her sister of eight years old, a game, and now two children what expansiveness!

Evie . . .

I sit alone and no one visits me. I think I remember family but that was thirty years ago. A dad, a basic man, and a mom, who felt defective and ashamed of herself because of my birth and conditions. I am blind and mentally retarded. I am a ward of the state. In my mind, I am free to think in small and constrained ways. They feed me and clothe me, but take me nowhere. I think I had some brothers and sisters, and they never came to see me after a while. I was an embarrassment to them. So, I sit and look at the little birdies in the trees outside the group home where I have lived so long. I have a boy friend but I am not sure what that means really. I survive at a level and I wonder what improvement I would have made if someone talked to me daily for years. I may be retarded but I m not stupid. My sister discovered me about four yeas ago, and a lot has changed. I am getting to know her and love her. My life has been dramatically changed since she came into my life. My going out has increased, my verbal skill has increased, my clothing style is more contemporary and the food got better too! Do you know how angels are standing around us all the time? I can see them as they have been with me since I was born. The Angel Gabrielle told me that my purpose in life was to grant full love and family to my sister when she was ready. I have achieved that goal and I have enjoyed my discovery of her too. She is funny, has a lot of energy, and I think I balance her out. Her life has changed because of me. She is the mother I never had and my sister. Sometimes I am little and need a mom. We love each other very much and I put her in my will. It says that she receives the blessings of the Father, Son, and the Holy Spirit and all the goodness and love I have to leave. I'll be in heaven—don't worry . . .

Harry . . .

Bemused and enjoying life, he is in inner torment and joy. Can I be a man independent and connected at the same time? Can I let go of my son? What will happen to him and to me? I have loved him into through and out of his pain. Some of it is mine, I know. My son! My son! My son! I realize my dreams for him died long ago, that's ok but his young heart, his young brave heart. I love him more than words can tell. I have worried countless times, and in depth. I tell you, it has almost broken me. God gives me strength. How I could have collapsed but no, no, not in front of or because of my son. He can't know this. I need to be strong. Somewhere he needs to see it as I think he seldom sees it in himself. Help me to see that I can heal him or someone! In some way! My heart needs a slight glimpse before I weaken too. I support his growing and leaving. I will wonder how he is doing forever and ever. I once had a 'why me', but now I know my own inner blessings and now have a 'yes I am able' with deep love, compassion, and honor to a gentler soul.

Iris . . .

I made this! . . . and this!! . . . and this too!. I'm impressed as Iris passes before me her creative designs of trays, ashtrays, Halloween figures in assorted colors, and other pieces of various shapes and sizes. She is eight years old a little girl laughing as she throws herself over the living room couch in an acrobatic circus style move. Energy, energy, energy. Out the door to the little park with friends to run around making up games only children can. Striking eyes and blond hair flying about. I do not want anymore she says of the entrecote on her plate. Ximo says eat more it is good for you. Crime Scene Investigator, Iris Tarrega Soler, professional specialist inspects the tiny red mark on the table. Is it cherry juice or maybe human blood? Don't anybody touch it she commands. The observers obey her because they know she is intensely busy at work now utilizing her medical forensic science mind to help solve these difficult criminal cases. She has successfully solved many complex, puzzling situations and is so good as a CSI that the United States of America is considering bringing her to several universities as a visiting lecturer. She is world renown for her work. Oh, and by the way, the red mark on the table was cherry juice.

Jim . . .

Gay, he knew it, he knew it all along, since childhood. Very intelligent too-a good thing, because he could figure people out fast to protect himself and his differences that leaked. Near to being shunned by his father, and definitely by his brother, he lived on loyal to his family and thought in time they would change and accept him. His mother was his support, but oddly enough, his aunt was more so. She taught him so many things and he had so many questions to ask that they bonded in an emotional, intellectual way that nourished both deeply and spiritually. He did not let on as long as he could control it of his orientation. He played with the other kids, in the nearby hills to home. Running around on summer days and nights making up games and sleighing down the hill in wintertime for more fun. He fell in love with cooking at a very young age, doing it both at home and at his aunt's house. He saw his father make wine and in this comprehensive way he developed a taste for fine food and wine which today he shares his knowledge with others. He had learned to drive a car by the time he was 14 years old. He intended to become a doctor, or let's say it was intended for him, but he felt it not to be right for his inner heart and soul. Yes, he worked in a hospital and was excellent in and taught biology and chemistry, but he grew into his own truth, that of not wanting to be a doctor but to be in the helping profession nevertheless. A mini crisis of identity proved to be beneficial as he decided to become a psychotherapist, one who would develop a life working with others. His passion for learning continued as he sought to improve himself as a therapist in every way. He dedicated yearly time to it in a deep committed way. His sense of humor and play was a special gift. It was rumored that he had a collection of over 3000 jokes. He also was an avid collector of cookbooks and oriental rugs. It was known around town that if you could not find a recipe, he was the one to consult.

His hope that his father and brother who had ignored him came true in his later years. This was a spiritual gift to him, a healing he had hoped and longed for, and he could feel the gentle smile of his mother from Heaven, a smile that he felt into the depths of his heart mind and soul

John . . .

Here I am alone inside, not knowing to whom I belong. Why did I ever seek them out? They are crazy! My biological father tried to kill me—he told me and that is one reason I was put up for adoption. Now I'm just plain confused about my adoptive parents, my biological parents and myself. Who am I? My adoptive parents whom I love are great, they brought me up in the upper middle class and my biological parents live just above poverty. I have the upbringing of one and the genes of the other. I was told that not knowing was not good, no one ever said that knowing is not good. I can't express myself but I sure can get whatever I want. I'm very clever, some would say—a liar. I take—some would say I'm a thief. I set fires—some would say an arsonist. And . . . I get away with it all. I can't explain why my insides and my outer behavior are so disconnected but I think my inner life is ruled by my adoptive family and my outer life is ruled by my biological family. All three of these dimensions are at anti forces to each other. I want all of them and I don't want them, the two "themes" want me and don't want me. And all of this wanting goes on in an unidentifiable alternating pattern of crazy making intensity. Suicide is a possibility and so is healing but I can't choose between these two forces pulling in me either. There is a war for my soul, God and the Demon fighting on the soil of my soul, each unwittingly ignoring most of me and to the victor go all the spoils of which I am many. Spiritual confusion and loneliness, broken heartedness, despair, dread, depression and anxiety is what the winner gets. I am so conflicted . . .

Mame . . .

Ha ha ha! A drive by shooting but not with a gun, with my camera eye. So that is where she lived all those years with the secret. A middle class house where middle class events occurred. I am part of the secret, one that still lives on. I wonder if she thinks of me and the deed we share. I haven't seen her since that birthday. I wonder has she changed, what does she look like now and why is it that she doesn't want to see me? I respect her wishes but we are two adults now and maybe we can talk about it. She must be in pain, as I know that I am. Well I continue to drive on by. Maybe I'll come up this way again, but before I leave this time, I'll drive by her childhood home. My heart begins to hurt a bit not deeply yet, just the beginning of going there. My tears start forming like visual pills getting ready to come out my eyes and down my outsides slowly leaving mascara traces of pain and not loved ness. I should dare to talk to her but I can't. I am fearful of another rejection. Rejection at birth and rejection reaching out now as an adult to my mother is too much. What if I called her Mommy and she said no.

Marie . . .

It is true I am lessened by his death. I can't reconcile it all . . . It should have been me, not my lovely, luscious boy. So what you see is less of me, yes. My heart is broken and I can't repair it. I can live with it till I die when I will be reunited with him. My love for others still flows strongly. This is important to me and is not new to me, yet it fills me. I wonder if I had loved him a bit more beyond my abilities, would he be alive now. I'll never know. Did my admonishments get to him in a way that he translated as love—that's how I meant it. Does he know how much he is missed? He was always missed, I am sure he knows. What part of him that I did not know overtook him and overruled me? Do we all have a part that can be so dominant of us, if given the chance, and it even can take us over? I must say yes, with anger and despair I say it. What is my responsibility? They say none but only mothers know that feeling, culpable and guilty. In my heart, I know I am partly to blame or if I had been different all those years—if only, if only . . . I know it is a nutty thing but don't you see, it keeps me in conversation with him and we need that. After all he is my boy and I am his mom—forever.

Mark . . .

I am stunned! He told me about her. I am shocked and still reeling! I never knew. I am confused. What was past is now to be looked at differently. Her distance can be explained. Her not connecting with me can be explained. My tormented and tumultuous early years have different meanings now. My heart hurts for her and understands her offness. How damaged she must be and feel. Abuse of that kind, depth, and time is incurably destructive. Therapy cannot help. Those lovely hollow, vacant eyes the windows to her soul, yes to that soul I missed her true soul I think as much as she did but I thought I was getting the real thing now I know, no. What about my own soul? Is it also tampered with in a way and not fully here? My heart is open mostly but my soul I do not know. Where do I go from here and what do I say to her? I always felt but couldn't quite trust the deep and fleeting feeling I had that something was wrong. Almost invisible it would pass so fast. This piece of news makes the feeling visible, hearable, feelable and it is big. I turn to my wife, my loving wife, my partner and there is comfort there. I am sure that there are no other secrets and we all can move on better for the truth. My daughter will not suffer any secrets from me. I am going to see her now.

Moni . . .

Deep, wise, a soul. She loved life in that way. She understood the complexities, paradoxes, and conflicts. The story, that happening, surreal and loving, open and frightening, professional and personal, right and wrong, all intermingled in a yes spiritual way. I was not able she knew and thus this event had to happen. I kept it prized for many years-exactly because of the odd yet correct process. How did it affect me? I think it gave me an understanding that few people have, an entry into a forbidden area and I came out unharmed. The gift I received, one of the most profound, pure, was an event that few pass through not traumatized. I know of only traumatized ones, but not me. The times were different then and everyone knew their place governed by roles, ethics, and vulnerabilities unforeseen yet dealt with appropriately. Nowadays this kind of thing would create tragedies to all who know. So rest my soul in peace? A resounding yes to my soul to my self and to my life! And yes to him, the saving one.

Patricia . . .

A strong radiance, a deep knowing. Is this I? Do I portray something else more true about me? Can they see my laughter and fun polar to my suffering and pain? Do they know how I've endured and been to Life's death edge with him? Do they know that I know what it means to hold the hand of a tender soul at Death's door and to see one foot pass thru tentatively and to come back again? Do they know how many times I have done that? What mystery my life has been. How profound my times. I have not been able too much to let out and receive from others all that I need. I have to be strong, little do they know how hurt my heart is and I cannot tell the depth of it all to anyone. Not that is there is no one there, but my words fall short of the immensity of it all. The ache that goes to my cells no one will know, the fear that I cannot hide from, the wondering of the outcome so many times assured about a coin toss really. He has taught me how to survive and live even with a soul's question mark in front of him and me. How will he go on without me-I know he will—but almost—how dare he! I smile, I am not his God, but how will I go on without him?

Peter . . .

Strong, tall, kind, with a feeling of sensitivity. He comes from a complicated family and has one of his own. He married a Filipino woman. She juxtaposed his calmness with a certain quick jitteriness that could be engaging and off putting depending where you yourself were at emotionally. They had one son who they loved very much and who was a mix of the two. You could see Peter in his face along with some traces of grandparents. Peter would venture forth in this work somewhat anxious and curious. He truly loved the work and its providing discoveries. He would open to the new with an adult expectancy and a boyhood heart, well sometimes. He grew a lot over the year and became steadily open and sensitive. I imagined this helped him in his work but he never said and I never asked. What a great smile he has, one that captures you and welcomes you into his space. His support of others is evidenced by his willing participation and clarity of his way. He could speak for so many persons that the others called on him often.

That Blind Girl There . . .

At the home, four loving people lived innocuously. Some had even been there so long that the attendants did not know who or how they had been left off. I suppose they could look it up but no one thought to do that. One woman, retarded and blind, had been there the longest. She was admired by the other people in their simple way for having been so. Many vacant years-no one came to see her-she spent hidden in her mental chambers. Almost discarded by her mother, her father protested but he didn't win, she was put into this home at a young age. The mother, with deep pain, could hardly let her go at the time too. She knew it was best for her. The mother then turned her back and never looked after her daughter again. Slowly, over time, this made the mother bitter and disturbed. She could not believe that her sex could produce anything less than normal-but it did. It was a major blow to her self image. For many years this woman in the home hoped that some day someone would come and see her. She had trouble forming thoughts and images—she remembered her dad and strawberries—a cherished picture. Because of her retardation, she could not think very clearly about things but she had the greatest gift of all-the purity of love. And that was what she didn't know that was developing over the years, a love of all, and a simple grace unfolding. Would someone come she wondered in her quiet mind. Then, one day, someone came like angel proclaiming the arrival of Jesus and Salvation. A sister!! A sister??! I know what that means though I may not convey it well. Take me where? To pizza and ice cream and even to her house!? My dreams have come true and I m truly home now-I have family in my sister. From my little bit, can I convey to her my deep love and gratitude for coming to me? Can I convey to her that she is my angel? I hope she knows I can't find the word sometimes. I am blessed and believe me my god has answered my prayers.

The Attacked . . .

First into his head, then into his heart, then into his lungs, then into his gut goes the plunging carefully cared for knife. At first I did not know what hit me in the head and then I saw the knife in his hand as it made a beeline for my heart. I went numb with a quizzical do I know you look on my face. Haven't we met before, no? Well, shouldn't we introduce our selves? Gasping for air but still standing as I do not want to go down and I was a pretty good running back in my day, I let out or I mean my body lets out a terrifying moan-clearly not me as I am a quiet witness here, that's all. When I tried to lift my arms in defense, they would not come up. So fast was this gentleman with the knife that I was powerless. Next, he went into my gut, geez, I just ate. I better offer him my billfold and we both can go on about our lives. Where are my emotions? I am usually good and appropriate with my anger and my sadness but neither is present. Oh My God! The man is wearing a hat! Wait till I tell my friends. I am reluctantly sinking to the ground in a slow motion ballet of some kind. The man tips his hat! Can you believe it? Here he just punched me with his knife and he tips his hat!!?? Lying on the ground, I have always loved the ground, its support and what comes from it. You know I always thought I would die in bed, another kind of ground for me. Well, how can you know? Here I am in the street in front of a gentleman wearing a hat! So much for going out for a bottle of wine! Thank you very much!! Do you know how this will affect my life? I mean I have two kids and a wife. And how will it affect your life? You will be sorry soon I bet. I've always been a forgiving soul and now am no exception. Do you think I am foolish? I am just an ordinary American person who died with a bottle of wine in his hand, red wine, of course.

The Cat Lady . . .

In the town there is a woman referred to as the Cat Lady. Known to name her cats after literary persons and photographic equipment, she was said to be involved in those fields in some way. She would walk the town's evening glow streets with her cats oddly following right beside her as if on guard for her and her safety. She would walk the same path night after night perhaps looking for some relief from the inner movements that surged her. Her only item from the local pharmacist was Prozac, given—it was rumored—to help her bear her heavy workload. She also was a member of the town's political group. Leading many of the discussions that often occurred, she was asked to be the first selectman, but she did not want the responsibility, to lose time from her home, and to be away from her cats too much. She is politically astute, and volunteers much of her time, especially to the people at the neurological complex on the outskirts of town. She particularly liked Dr. Joe whom she had met many years before and she felt she knew and understood a lot about him. She wondered if the time she panicked on the bus, and one other time, were similar events to what precipitated Dr. Joe's fall but that she may have been stronger. She grew up loving Mother Nature, the forests, hills and waters, particularly the ocean. Nurturance she drew from there, a place perhaps, Dr. Joe did not have. Her mother was a very sexual woman and it was whispered that she had been seen in Dr. Joe's father's cobbler shop. The mother was not available for her daughter or any of her children, more wanting to experience life on her own as if childless and single. So the Cat Lady developed her own self, in her own way, becoming her own person. She also felt strongly that if not for her God watching over her, she would be in the complex. One man in the complex she believed did not belong there although he had murdered his girlfriend in a crime of passion. She enjoyed talking to him and found him fascinating and had some curious feelings for him too. The male nurse, the

African American, would often make passes at her when she came to visit, but she knew he was married and did not want or need the possible trouble that can brew. Besides, there was a man on the Town Council to whom she was drawn, and she could not tell if the feeling was mutual or not. She really liked him and could not discern his feeling though he was very warm and happy to see her each time. Well, time will tell she thought and I am not going to let on anything unless or until he does too. I have plenty to occupy me what with all my arts and crafts and my newfound responsibility for my sister who is blind and retarded. Finding her after all these years gave the Cat Lady a feeling of essence in the family for the first time. She was a fierce defender of her sister's rights and of the other's where her sister lived. Something of the Cat Lady grew into a tiger when sister matters were not clear nor well done. So, yes, busy with a heavy workload yet available to all who needed her, and loving her life and all those that came into it with compassion, laughter, joy, and freedom. She was well known and liked in the town, and other than her habitual night time evening walks, she was a free spirit, and proud. Rumor has it that she will be selected to lead the schools of the town, something she is prepared, willing and able to do.

The Cats . . .

Any one person does not own the Cats in the town. It is truly odd but the Cats belong to the town and it feeds them through the scraps from the restaurants, bars, and grocery store. The Vet does the 'fixing' so that they do not get out of control and reproduce too many Cats. Rumor is that the first Cat came with a female partner and he wasted no time in learning how to survey the town for its best eateries and to become special. King Cat as he became to be known was essentially father of all the other Cats. He would get his choices of food before the others and was careful to be a good role model so that no one Cat became overweight. Some townsfolk laughed and wondered if they could ask king Cat for his diet plan. King was black and a great leader and he spoke (meowed) to his constituency exhorting them on to be clean, safe and productive. So some Cats became in control of the rat division and others of the mouse control division. Others were responsible for annoying some of the more bold dogs in town in order to tire them out for their owners in the evening. Some had the luxury job of making themselves available for petting by the people in the town. King cat meowed that it would be best to keep a low profile in town and all agreed.

The Chief . . .

I'll fix the bastards! They are not going to screw me up! Not me. I am the Chief of this town and no motorcycle bums are going to rest even overnight here as far as I am concerned. I gave the word and it successfully got out. Anyone breaking the noise ordinance would get thrown onto his ass and into jail. I worked hard to get to where I am and I came up thru and paid my dues to the force. We are a small department only totaling twenty-one officers, two sergeants, two detectives and myself. So we have everything under control here in town. Over the years I have made several nice arrangements with some of the townsfolk and although bordering on the illegal, everyone seemed happy and satisfied with their involvement. One such situation which is a little more risky than the others is my visits to the store run by the florist in town. She happens to have an 'arrangement' upstairs that I frequently take part in. There is one young girl there that I take a fancy to but I do not want her to know about it. She knows my position in town and let's say we have an unspoken agreement that benefits the both of us. I saw her in town on a few occasions and I pretend I do not know her. I recently asked her if I could meet her when she got of work and she graciously declined. I was surprised at how hurt I felt. I suppose there is an ethics which she must be following. Also any more involvement could get me into trouble. My wife who is a good person doesn't know about these extracurricular activities and I feel it has affected our togetherness in a significant way. I just wish to be unencumbered in sex and a little unknown and she would not understand that. We have been married forty years and we have three grandchildren who do not live nearby I am very happy with her except for this one peccadillo of mine. I am conservative, repressed in my ways and for me to go though the Florist's is very bold of me, and I do not want to get caught. I'll make sure that does not happen. I would have to move to another town and I love it here.

The Day The Clothing Shop Closed . . .

Suits and shirts, and blouses with empty men and women and unfilled underpants, shoes and socks plus many other items one finds in such a store.

All the stuff here made somewhere else by foreign hands to be worn by local bodies, strange . . . The owner was very happy with her little store here in town. It had once been a pet store and when she bought it, it took 3 cleanings to get rid of the smells. But she succeeded and now it smelled of lavenders and roses and other 'for sale' scents. She also had background music on all the time, which bothered one customer in particular. She had come from a town in the Midwest where she had murdered her store partner with knitting needles, scissors and other sharp objects. She spent ten years in prison for her deed and when she got out came to this little town to start anew. There were other people in the town who had done time and, as it was a strange little town, it often drew in kinds of people like these. The young man who was following her was the son of the woman she killed. He planned to return the favor to her daughter. 'How' was the problem and he had not done such a thing before. He had killed little animals like cats and dogs but this is a human being. Plus he did not want to get caught and be in jail like this woman had been. So in a quandary, he decided he would have some jail time for the act of how he would kill her, and he may even get away with it.

He decided to run her down with his car. He noticed that she always parked in the same place across the street every day and that if he did it right he could nip her in the bud and probably get 'running from the scene of the accident as his crime'. So he practiced everyday and felt he could catch her in the middle of the street at the right time. He had scared some of the walkers who came into the path he would follow. He felt guilty about that but he needed the practice and did not really hurt anyone. He would watch her coming out of the clothing store and thought he might like to fuck her too, but that might get him too close and off his purpose. She dressed well as she should but she does not know which outfit she will wear on her dying day. He would know. So he takes a walk by the store and decides to look in the window at her. She smiled a bit, but she would not recognize her taker. He decided on a Wednesday. He had always wondered about the 'wed' at the beginning of the word. A ceremonial beginning, and a ceremonial end for her on Death day. So here it is, can he really do this? He had a few drinks to numb himself out. There she comes out of the store on this beautiful sunny day, blue skies, and pleasant breezes, and motor running.

As she carelessly steps into the street moving towards the middle, the young man, as he had practiced before, stepped on the gas and the engine responded perfectly and off he went on his mission. Smashing into her had a silent and yet loud sound. She came up on the hood of the car with blood flinging itself onto the windshield in a slightly Christian cross configuration . . . odd. Continuing her ascent up over the top of the car she met death somewhere near her fall to the rear bumper. He could not have done better. A car drove in front of him and he had to stop behind it. Funny, he had not thought much about the consequences of the after accident.

He was charged with drunk driving and reckless endangerment. Being his first infraction he was put on house arrest for six months and probation for five years and one hundred hours of community service, not bad!

The Depressed One . . .

I'm not doing my job, I'm too depressed to do it. Something came over me like a dark foreboding blanket of doom. Thank God for the medicines. I know I'm letting my family down a lot but I try to do my best. Why did this depression hit me? I have a lovely wife and children for whom I have provided and now I'm functionally disabled. I can't concentrate nor focus on anything I attempt to do, not work things or even when I can try, play things. Sex totally is uninteresting to me and I am overeating all the time. Why can't I get control? So this is what the body can do to me after 50 years it goes awry chemically and I suffer the consequences of personal and interpersonal losses. Days drag slowly by like molasses through the hourglass of time, an endless end. Food has no taste but the medical mix of biochemical flowers overriding it. My motion seems pedantic and crestfallen—movements of a handicapped ballet performer. Arm to itch on the hand seems like I move my hand through a water air, slowly with deliberativeness to reach its mark and then to eventually return to my side as if forcing itself like a job against the wind. My thoughts come to me like a lobbed ball in tennis—slowly arching up and down rather than before when they came straight like a bullet from a rifle. My eyeballs move and scan in slow motion too. If I had to move first I would suffer from not doing it. My breath I seem to have to consciously pull it from my surroundings and then push it back into the world slowly like moving a refrigerator by myself. Colors are muted mostly pastel and pasty looking nothing vivid. Sounds are all in waltz time dancing towards me reluctantly. Smells are all the same, no clarity of one over another. Sleep takes me, sliding me into its grip without announcement and then providing me with no reasonable direction in dreams or nightmares. I don't care to dress well anymore or even to shower and shave—where would I go? Who would receive me anyway? At least I don't have to be in the Complex on the outskirts of this town. Please I hope to never be there, they are all crazy! They all have done something bizarre, me, I'm just so terribly depressed.

The Desk Clerk . . .

Wait, wait, wait. Just like on my job. Who is next to come through the door and when-its when that is the wait. But this is different, new. I am waiting for her to arrive. She usually comes late for our meeting but it always turns out all right. She is Korean and works at the neurological complex on the outskirts of town and we hit it off right away when we met at the pharmacy three times in a row. I said did she want to get a coffee and she said yes in her accented way. Her beigey, coffee and cream coloring caught my eye and pulled me in for a drink. She was a tan yellow color if you can visualize what I mean. After coffee she asked me back to her house where her family would not be home. We realized that we both work at the Complex at different ends of the campus, and could probably explain anything we might need to do. At her house she brought me into her bedroom and undressed me and made love to me in a beautiful and I think Geisha sort of way. She was like a little kid after it-playful as hell. It released a different kind of energy in her and she wanted me to play too. I am not too spontaneous but her little girl showing up on the outside invited my little boy to come to the surface and play too. I thought I could have a relationship with her but I did not know what she might think. She slowly dressed giving me a reverse strip tease. I loved it. She seemed ready and in a hurry to go from the house—probably someone due home. Back at my car she gave me a little reassuring tap from the playful side and then became so grown up in front of my eyes that it surprised me. When saying goodbye she seemed already on her way in her mind about five minutes ago but she did give me her number as she went off to work.

The Dog on the Table

How did he get there—this dog on the table? He must have jumped up onto the couch and then walked onto the table to sprawl beside the lamp. Watching him breathe in the lamp air and tasting the light and smelling the all about him made me stop and stare. At first he sat like a regal figure then he lay down like a sphinx. What was he thinking? Probably, look at me aren't I the cutest thing in your field of vision? About eight pounds, brown, black, and white hair covered his shihtzu body. The light of the lamp highlighted his white hair making him distinguished and looking a bit like Robert Frost. He made little sounds like half bark, half whine in some sort of plea. Come and get me may be the message or something else may be the goal. Probably some good old attention and time. Play with me don't leave me alone too long. Now, head down on the table sleep time. No, his eyes are open, watchful, and sweet just like his ancestors have done in Tibet. What if he is pondering my existence as a person and human being? What does he perceive? More than a caretaker I am sure. I impose into his view a sense of admiration and love and compassion. He wonders how I get along on just two feet and would I be fast enough in running if I had to. He knows he is faster than me. He also ponders the voice making sounds I create and why he can't understand them and why I can't understand him. Yet across this mystery, a communication occurs. He can't sort out why I put on clothing rather than just going off to work but he also knows my hair is not long enough to keep me warm. Still he wonders why I don't have the hair.

The Druggist . . .

Well no harm done, just a little skimming off the top. Didn't butchers used to put their thumbs on the scales when weighing the meats? This purchaser won't know the difference in milligrams anyway. Most of them never check the written information either so in a way it is their fault not mine. The one time I did do the reverse I overdid a prescription cause the customer has always been a pain in the ass and I thought I might accidentally, let's say, screw up his system. What I have most difficulty with is my own addiction and for a pharmacist this is difficult to deal with as the drugs are always there. I do have a bit of will power and only go so far. I just have to finagle with the paper work to come out right. I am sure you know how I make things balance already. Living in this boring town with these weird people, I need to get high often for the stimulation. The kaleidoscope of colors that I see makes me happy. Mostly though I need them for my visits to the Florist's place, a place of refuge and fun. I have an arrangement with her and some of her girls that benefits all concerned. I get free nights whenever I want in exchange for some valiums, percosets and some other not too dangerous drugs. I also happen to have a small field behind my store where I grow some stuff very easily. As I am an upstanding member of the community no one suspects me. I'm a good person of course.

The Florist . . .

She came to town unannounced but noticed. She bought the old florist shop and modernized and contemporized the inside really well to match the colorful flower arrangements she did herself. Round, triangle, and crescent, taken to new visions by her creative spirit and just plain sense good eye for beauty. She was a bit of a beauty herself, dressing smartly and well. She had come from the city fifteen miles away after a difficult divorce with an attorney husband-no children but him she would say. Her business picked up where the previous owners left off and her flair drew in more customers. The Director of the Complex seemed to take a fancy to her though he could not explain it, it was only biological and he had made a decision. The florist, also had, secretly, begun a high-class escort service in the rooms above her shop. It was very discreet, well appointed and expensive. The chief of police was a subscriber, so she had protection as well. Her favorite flowers were the carnations and she would, on occasion, send a bunch to the neighboring shops to beautify the stores. She, once while still in the city nearby, made a bed of carnations-red and white—for her boyfriend and her pleasures. One thing, she loved sex and in all positions! She also had joined the Mile High club a couple of times. Raised a catholic, she even considered going to church again after seeing and hearing about the handsome priest. She decided against it-wrong reasons. The Director of the Neurological Complex was handsome too she noted and she could feel his attention to her in a shy way. So, for a few years now, she has done very well and planned on staying but needed a guy around. Some of the men had asked her out but none appealed to her that much and she hoped her luck might change. Soon, she would find it did.

The Girl in the Corner Apartment . . .

How I love it here in my apartment. I look down on Main Street on two sides and I can watch all the walker s and understandable incidents that occur. I work for the Florist in her—I hate to say—the word brothel, where I service anywhere from five to seven men per night. I get one hundred twenty five dollars out of the 200 dollar fee. I love my work too. I see a therapist who is probably learning a lot from me. When I told him I am a person, he reacted as if I am not. We talked about it and I can see he has some moral judgments about my work. He tends to think it has to do with my childhood, where as I think it has to do with the money. I earn a lot of it and I have a big savings account already. Many important townspeople come to see me, like the Chief of Police, a banker, a couple of prominent businessmen and many other non-repeaters. I think that the Chief has a crush on me of which I am happy about cause he could arrest me if he wanted. I have furnished my apartment well but not extravagantly, as I like to save money. I had been working in the grocery store when one day the Florist asked me if I would like to have my pay incredibly multiplied. I said yes of course but I do not know anything about flowers. To myself I thought a pyramid scheme of some kind. She asked if I had time for lunch that day, and I did. We met and after some formal chitchat, she asked me if I had a boyfriend. At the time I did not, but hopeful was between them. She questioned about how many I had had, and I said six. Next she began saying how much she enjoyed sex and men and did I? Feeling safe with her I told her my truth-yes very much!! Then she proceeded to tell me how she had worked for an escort service for some time and how it was very safe especially in small towns where secret s were well kept and that cell phones made things a lot easier too. The description intrigued me but I still did not know what was to come, as I am a bit naïve. Suddenly it dawned on me her comment this morning, multiplying my hourly wage.

She was asking me indirectly if I wanted to be a call girl! Indirectly, me too, I was answering yes on some unconscious level. So the ball must be in my court so I dared tell her that I would be interested in that kind of work too. I surprised myself but it felt right. The Florist opened up and told me what would be done, terms of money splitting, and then told me of the location which I knew but did not know what was happening there above the flower shop at night. I would be in the bedroom upstairs and the men would come in to see if they wanted to be with me, if I were the type they wanted. If not they would go to another room on their quest. Was I all right with rejection? Well I think so. If the man liked me he would tell me what he wanted, and I would bare myself and do whatever. I could stop at any time but let me tell you the money is so good that it keeps me into it and the work is not bad. Most of the men just want to hold me then get a blowjob.

Some men want to talk about all kinds of things. A few like me to slow dance in a striptease for them some do not even want sex. Anyway, the first night I was anxious. I was wearing a halter top with a jeans skirt and sandals and I looked pretty good. A man opened the door and my heart jumped! I was about to be arrested by the Chief of police! He entered the room and asked me my name which I changed to a different one, why I do not know as the Chief had come grocery shopping all the time and probably knew my real name. He moved over to the bed beside me and assured me I was not under arrest but that I could put the cuffs on him, it would please him. So we undressed and I cuffed him Now I'll call the police I laughed in my head. He wanted me to spank him, God I've never hit anyone in my life, but money is money so I gave him a good smack and he let out a yelp and asked for more slapping. I did it again and I started to feel angry-it was weird—as if he were disobeying me and I was punishing him. He began to get red on his bum after about forty whacks and I felt like Lizzie Borden. Next he wanted oral sex and this was my first test professionally, that is. I put the condom on him and began and I hoped he would come off quickly but that was not the case. As I began to tire and to sweat, it was difficult work; I stopped for a while to rest. It was then from out of the blue I was stunned by a slap of full force across my face so strong that I fell off the bed. A bit dazed, I felt these supportive arms around me saying I would be ok and not to worry. It was the Chief, I admitted later, that it gave me a different kind of sexual buzz, though I do not want it to happen again. He apologized, said it was revenge and he was still waiting his satisfaction. We began again and it took less time till he ejaculated into the condom with orgiastic, deep, rumbling sounds. Over and done and I felt pretty good except for being slapped. As he dressed and he was leaving he gave me a twenty-dollar bill for a tip and he said he'd see me again. I needed to do a lot of self-reflecting then. What a beginning and one hundred and seventy dollars for the hour! I'm going to continue the work or at least I will do next week too, The next man who looked in, came in too. I'm lucky, no passbys. He was a guy I had seen in the store several times, young cute guy who should have a girlfriend or maybe does. He wanted traditional sex so I had to just be normal and all was ok with him. Poor guy, premature and embarrassed about it but I'll not say anything except be positive. That issue is what he wants to overcome and could I help. Yes I thought if you have a million dollars to spare. So he ended the session well and he said he wanted to see me again. The next man truly shocked me because he was African American, which for some reason I did not expect in this little town and in this expensive business. But after my shock, which he also noted, I was able to do my job. I observed that it is blacker than the rest of the body, which surprised me too. I was exhausted and energized at the same time. I probably would not sleep when I got back to my apartment. I am supposed to be here till two am, which is real late for this town, but I can manage it. The fourth guy has a foot fetish and wanted to masturbate and lick my feet at the same time. This one I like, it is easy in me. The one thing about it is that I had to control my laughter even though he said it was quite all right. So this was my first night. It was not hard at all and I made six hundred and seventy dollars in five hours and the next morning I quit the grocery store job. When I went home that night I was so energized I could not sleep until five and then I awakened at eleven am wondering if it was a dream, I felt clean and safe, and ok in my head too. I wonder what tonight will bring. I quit my job and bumped into my mom around three pm and we went for a coffee. I wanted to tell her but of course I would not. I again wondered if she loved sex or not. Later that afternoon, I took a nap and signed up at the gym as I think I am going to have to have a good wind and strength. Thinking of my mother I wonder what she would say, maybe good for you or go to hell. I am also thinking that she was once very pretty when younger and probably had a good figure and would have been good at this kind of work. Oh well. I'll never know. Back to work again tonight and I felt a bit of glee to be going again, I think cause of the money. So my first door opener tonight, closed it after seeing me-a rejection. I hope this is not going to be my night, the second door opener came in and stayed. He wanted to talk first. Questions like why do you do this and how long will you and do you like it all the time-a barrage actually. I answered him and he did get me thinking I am twenty-four and I figured in ten years, if I stay in it that long after normal expenditures I could have about one million dollars saved. That would be good for the rest of my life, as I am prudent with my spending. Soon he wanted me to masturbate him and that was all. He had a ring on and I thought he was probably married and out playing. The rest of the night was uneventful and fairly ordinary. After the second night upon walking home, my last customer seemed to be following me. Soon though he took a different turn, and was no longer behind me. It gave me a weird feeling. Once at the apartment I felt home and safe. I was not as energized as the first night so sleep came a little easier. I did have the thought of sex without love and it lingered with me for a while. It is what men do I conjectured. I wondered what sex would be like with my father. Is he premature or does he do oral-ugh-stop these thoughts! Or my brother! Well he has seen me naked and I him, sort of a nonverbal gesture in the bathroom hallway when we were teens. I kind of liked showing him my body though we never talked about it-too ashamed or maybe too hot. My religion as I have very little of it does not interfere with my thinking or being, in other words, I do not feel guilty about it In fact I think what I do is good for the men I see. At least they all feel good about it and I serve some primal need of humankind and I am thinking of being a geisha girl where I would put the man into a sauna, then give him a table shower, then deep massage with a happy ending. I would dress in those kimonos of beautiful colors and paint my face white and I would feel more legitimate too. I could get arrested but as long as the Chief is OK with it, I think I am safe. He comes once a week for the little games we play of bondage and discipline and we enjoy it. When I see him in the streets he completely ignores me but at the business he is all attentive. Weird, huh? So, I have some regulars and some new ones every night. And I make a nice pay as I said before.

The Grateful Dead . . .

When I first did it I could not explain me to myself. It felt good and that is all I cared about. The 'G' string was the best one to use as I had tried the others but they were either too thick or too thin. The fear explored up my back in a coffee spill kind of way each time—but it felt good. A little kitten was the first. I laugh now as I think of how frightened I was at the volume of sound it made dangling at the end of my guitar 'G' string garrote. So, yes I did several other small animals and a couple of big dogs because I knew for what I was rehearsing. I loved the music the guitar-basically wood and wire,—could make. I sing all the songs of the 60's and 70's and have a small following in Manhattan at some of the clubs. I seem to play with more gusto after killing someone. It must be the remnant rush from the act. My first human was a kid from the Bronx and I was 15 at the time. I just didn't like him, the way he walked, some kind of handicap. I came up behind him on one Fall day. It may have been late September. I wish I could remember. Anyway I snapped the wire around his neck with speed, clarity, and strength. It was a used 'G' string so I did not mind the blood and the 'inside of the neck' stuff on it. I suppose his flailing arms made it a bit more difficult than I expected but I learned a lot from him, being my first human. I could get a sense, although general, of how most may react. I've done it so many times in various parts of the City and I sing and write songs about them too. I watch the stupid motherfuckers listening to me singing with fucked up grins and smiles. They don't know that I am actually telling my truth. Here is a song:

> I walked through the City one morning
> Down a dusty side street of pain
> There I met a young man

Who was under some strain
I killed him on the spot
And that was the gain

Chorus:
Oh how grateful are the dead
Upon lovingly losing their head
What a soft space I have in my heart
I only kill people I don't know a lot

Continuing along the alleys of town
I met a young girl who was selling herself
As I asked to see her back and her ass
I snapped off her head with style, grace and class
There she shrieked and I ran as I heard a voice
I got a bit winded but I hadn't a choice

One funny thing happened where I almost got caught. I had not killed anyone in a while and it was a boring winter day. Everyone had on coats, which interfered with my fun. I had to restrict myself to drunks in the Bowery and bums I'd meet. They were asleep or too drunk to struggle and I was releasing them anyway. So, one late evening I saw a man standing by a streetlight and I decided to go for him. The damndest thing!! He had on one of those neck braces you wear after a fender bender. Now let me tell you I am tremendously strong in my arms and hands but this surprised the hell out of me The guy turned around with a frightened look as I drove my fist into his nose. I am sure I broke it. He fell backwards into the street. I skedaddled right out of there as I was sure he really did not see me and I didn't want to hurt him any more than I had already. Let's see if I can figure it out. I have been doing this for about 20 years and I must have killed 55 to 60 people. I am sure you don't believe me but that is your issue. When I am singing to the foolish crowds, it is like my confessional there. I also know that the dead are grateful for the release. I have written many songs with death being the main issue. I realized how ironic it was when I killed one of my own audience persons. I just got a glimpse of the side of his face but my wire was already doing its job.

I have to be careful. I have to have control. I have to choose more carefully, more wisely. I don't want to kill my own business!

The Gym Teacher

The gym teacher, a golden California-type boy of twenty-four years, had been sexing the seniors at the school in town for three years now, just when he began teaching. The girls, all daughters of the people of the town, were adorable one and all. These seventeen-year-old beauties were perfect and nubile, ripe and ready. The high school boys were no match for the perceived maturity of the gym teacher. The girls were perfectly OK with the knowledge of this thirst and hunger for female completions, as long as each one had a turn with him. He would introduce them to the tantric principles of love, although in reality it is a method for older sexuals. He loved the sight of the young girls' nipples and vaginas so smooth and untrampled. An older woman showed the contact in her distressed body. Insatiable he is, and take take, take is his way. Yes, he uses a condom because mainly, he could go longer. He did not like coming back on his self rather than unioning with whatever girl but he did not need the complexity of pregnancy—he felt too young to be married. In fact, one time he did get a girl pregnant and she gave birth to a baby boy whom she gave up for adoption. He denied it was his and went to a lawyer to find out his rights. He didn't want anyone to know. Her father threatened to kill him. After a while, the gym teacher heard that the lawyer had been killed in a blow up in his boat—one less to know made him feel OK and guilty. But now that was five years in the past and this is now, a time for play with the girls who were willing in the town. Finally, one of the girls who felt she had been passed over had her father and brothers (after they found out) go and confront the gym teacher. His car tires, his apartment surroundings, and his feeling of safety were all lashed a little bit, as was he one bloody night in town.

The Hairdresser . . .

I love my job it is fantabulous! I love creating styles for women and the men especially. Though I don't have many of them come to me. I live in my apartment in town and I have it beautiful and so contemporary. I like pinks and light colors and they look good on me. I'm gay and cannot help it. In my twenties I prayed, sort out religious retreats, I had some women friends but everything I tried failed to keep me hetero. So, this is me now and I accept me. Many of the townsfolk do not accept me. One reason is the tone of my voice. I truly sound faggy and queer and I can't help it, I can't hide it. I have some great gal friends and we get together for dinner exchanges and I also have a boy friend but I mention him last because he is the newest in my life. He is glorious with a buff body, a big dick, and an M.D. degree. I met him on the way into a glory hole place in the nearby city. We spent the night talking together the whole time, and we have been together ever since. It's only three weeks but in the gay world that is a long time. He worships me and when I need my space, he gives it to me too. We go kayaking on the nearby river and do lots of physical outdoors things too. He works at the Neurological Complex on the outskirts of town. He is very non-gay in tone and gesture—you would never know. We get together for dinner with one of the girls here who lives in the corner apartment and she is always asking him health questions, but she is so nice we don't mind it. My customers all love me and think I'm a lot of fun. I do most of the women who own shops in town like the Florist, the Pet Storeowner and others. I can't go into the bars in the West end of town as I did once before. I was confronted, mocked, and almost got hit. If I hadn't mentioned that I probably did many of their girlfriends and mothers' hairdos, they might not have let me go. This is a strange town and I don't think I'll stay long here. New York city calls me. My M.D. boyfriend could change my plans as I think I am falling in love with him, and he with me. I suppose we could commute from the nearby city to work here. We'll see. He may not stay at the complex too long either. So I'm a little uncertain about my love in the future.

The Liquor Store Owner . . .

Pints, half pints, quarts, the store had all kinds of bottles. He had owned the store for only two years but he had seen the profits grow even in this short time. Coming from a far away state he chose this town to settle in as he thought that no one would know or check into his past. So far, so good. A long time ago he had a weird life. He shot his next-door neighbor because the neighbor's dogs were always running wild and one of them killed his puppy of six months. He could not explain his behavior nor what made him go buy the gun-something he actually feared to own for the reason of the existence of guns to shoot something or someone. He was possessed and acted normally at the same time. He could watch himself while being possessed and could do nothing about it. This behavior emerged as being out of his control. He understood how some murderers were able to do it and not have any remorse. Having your body be used for some thing you would not choose is an overwhelming process. Well, he served his time, fifteen years, and still felt he did the right thing. He liked the town and its inhabitants a lot of whom are a bit quirky and a little off he amusingly thought . . .

The Masochistic Jogger . . .

Running, running, running. When will I stop? Maybe eight miles, maybe 10, today. I run like the Indians: I don't move my arms and it looks like I'm sitting down. I can go far as I save all that arm energy for my legs. People laugh at me. I had learned how to run like this at a Wilderness Camp I went to. My teacher, my master, would beat me with his fists until I bled, moaned, and almost passed out. Truth told, I liked it. It was frightening, exciting, dangerous, and put me close to death in an odd way in my mind. It also made me feel so alive. I did not report him, though I was only fifteen the first time it happened. It was in the woods, far from the camp, when he came upon me. I had been running about four miles up to that point. Sweating sexual beadlets of desire, sexual moistness spreading down my legs—why else run? He stopped me and I knew he could smell my youth, passion, and confusion all at the same time. He slapped me hard across the face and I saw stars and felt an orgasm, too. Next he punched me in the stomach and I bent over moaning for more—I'm just a kid!! Pulling my running shorts down from behind and sliding my panties to the side, he plunged into my sexual outlet with a primitive, healing male passion. I would birth the Devil himself. Again he slapped my behind so hard he almost jarred himself loose, and I orgasmed again from some deep prehistoric depth unknown to many. Anger in me began to arouse, but anger of the animalistic it is OK kind rather than the I'm insulted kind. Next he came with such a force I believed I felt it at the back of my throat and spit out. Finally he kneed me in the shoulder and I fell to the ground, my Mother, looking at the sky, my Father and feeling nothing but aliveness in every cell of my body. Sipping my own blood, aching in many places, I smiled and fell asleep.

Upon awakening, the aches felt like pangs of humanness to me. Blue blood ribbon for savagery, red blood for sadism, and green blood for seduction—nothing pretty, but truly human. Kill me, kill me, kill me, I desired! Maybe next time. Now I'm twenty-eight and no one treats me that way anymore—all very civilized, you know. Only in the town in the West End do I sometimes feel like dying. It is the men there, strange . . .

The Pet Store Owner . . .

   She truly loved these little guys that is what she called her puppies and she felt a twinge of regret every time she sold one though she was in business to do just that. She had been in town many years and remembered the fire in which one of her 'guys' died in, about 15 years ago. It was a lhasa apso, she remembered, a feisty little guy too. Lately, a gentleman has been coming to the store and she has had some very good talks with him about dogs and she found out that he is the Director of the Neurological Complex on the outskirts of town. She noticed a squint of a feeling from her to him and wondered what it would be like to go out with him. It is known that he is not married. He is interested in a small dog. He seems like he has a lot of love to give it seems also somehow locked up in there. Next time he comes in this will be the scene. He will go to the puppies and ask to hold one as usual. His face beams and he looks right into my eyes and I beam back at him. He then invites me to a drink at the tavern in town and I agree. We go to the bar and I order a White Russian in case I need to loosen and he orders a scotch on the rocks. We talk about pets for a while and he beams again and so do I. Fortunately, I can talk about the arts as my brother is an art critic in the city and I learned a lot from listening to him. By accident-true!—I bump his leg under the table, but at first I thought it was the table and I pushed more against it and it gave way. I was anxious and pushed it to relieve some anxiety and it was his leg! When I realized it, I became very embarrassed, as it actually was also a show of my aggression. He laughed and asked if I were a skier or a runner as I had such a strong leg. I told him neither and did I really push him away? He said did I want to try it again. I thoroughly deepened in purple face I am sure. I felt my leg go up against his though this time I could not move him, even while holding the table with both hands. It was so sexually exciting and flushing I did not know what to do with myself! He reached his hand over to mine and gently squeezed it and asked if I were ok. At that moment I knew, I knew he did not know much about women. It was clear in my heart and it endeared him to me I thought well why not ask him to coffee at my place. He says yes but not for long as he needs to get back to the Complex and in fact why not just have coffee here? This made the twinge of puppy love come to me again. I thought go slow, so I did, coffee here is fine. We ordered and he talked about his job a bit but seemed more interested in mine. His charm was evident as was his listening ability. He would confirm and validate me often during the conversation. Soon he needed to go and he told me he needed a friend like me. I was really hurt, friend? I did not tell him, as I knew I would see him again. But this—as I said—was all a scene not real; I guess I made this scene because I still don't believe that I can get close to someone again not even in a fantasy way. A friend is just what I need too. I cannot love as I fear it and I fear its vulnerable invitation and the insecurities I feel. With my shop and my dogs I am in control and I like this very much. I m not good at picking men I pick ones who beat me up. So I just don't go out any more. I don't want to be hurt anymore and to tell you the truth I think before I wanted to be hurt because I thought so little of myself. No, no more. So I won't let these feelings develop for this man but I will continue interested.

The Town Drunk . . .

Vomiting yellow and greenish fluid and chunks hit the ground, possibly parts of the inside of the body. Some pink and black emissions too. No matter, the town drunk will go on nevertheless. Used soda bottles and soda cans and an old grocery store basket to fill will be my day's work. So many people do not bring back their empties, so I make out ok with enough change to buy my favorite cheap wine. In truth, I am just a shell waiting to die. Garbage in garbage out, Liquor in liquor out, that is my whole day. Since the death of my wife and child and the burning down of my house-they think I set it-life has no meaning. To see the charred remains of a life and a family, still rules me in my mind. All I see is fire, and death and destruction so I blot out the pictures there. Yes it was a murder I m sure, I had enemies. I am the former sheriff of the court in town and I gave many people subpoenas that did not want them, many angry people. So I am sick all the time. I am trying to kill myself it dawned on me the other day. Why is it taking so long? Why do I keep waking up every morning to live again? I open like a flower every day no choice just a reaction to the sun. I fear to kill myself directly, I just cannot do it. And who is the nurse who hangs around me every now and then? She says she wants me to be ok-who is she anyway? She says she works at the complex in town and wouldn't I like to spend some time there to get to feel better? No thank you, as feeling better means feeling the pain. She doesn't understand this. I think the person who burned my house down is in the complex.

The Druggist . . .

Well, no harm done, just a little skimming off the top. Didn't butchers used to put their thumbs on the scales when weighing the meats? This purchaser won't know the difference anyway. Most of them never check the written information either, so in a way it is their fault, not mine. The one time I did do the reverse, I overdid the prescription cause the customer was a pain in the ass, and I thought I might accidentally, let's say, screw up his system. What I have most difficulty is with my own addictions and for a pharmacist this is difficult to deal with as the drugs are always in front of me. I do have a bit of will power and only go so far I just have to finagle with the paperwork to get it to come out right. I am sure you know how I make things balance already. Living in this boring town with these weird people, I need to get high often for the stimulation. The kaleidoscope of colors that I see makes me happy. Mostly though, I need them for my visits to the Florist's place, a place of refuge and fun. I have an arrangement with her and some of her girls that benefits all concerned. I get free nights whenever I want in exchange for some valiums, percasetes and s some other not too dangerous drugs. I also happen to have a small field behind my somewhere I grow minor stuff very easily. As I am an up standing member of the community no one suspects me. I am a good person, of course.

Will . . .

How did I do all this? Ten children counting all the souls. Did I merit this from some past life deed? How was I to know that I had so much love? It surprises me and the children have changed me grandly. The twins, oh how they shine in me like angels in love. My heart opens wide to love and receive their love. How expansive I am and feel, though few know. I'm a mature man now and I have these little guys, I think to God, please, please, a long life!! Let me run well with them, let me walk in their shadows, let me be close and reverent with them as they grow. Let me watch their lives unfold till at least they are young adults. Please, their weddings?? They will live on and I will pass long before them. Please-I can watch them even after? Can I visit them in their dreams? Can I have them join me when it is their time? Can I be with all ten surrounding me as their father? Can we dance and sing the songs we used to sing, and run on the beach, and play cards and games and with toys and be angels of joy for You? Let each unique soul that I have in my heart-I have a big heart—and I have in my life, be radiant, loving and free. Let me see, let me hear, let me know You thru them and them thru You. Thank you for this gift of souls for whom I hope I have served You well, for to whom much is given, much is expected. I propose to you an A plus for myself in fathering.

Thank You

Hospital People and
Some Others

Struggling to be Free . . .

He stood still and inside could feel himself struggling to be free. He already knew that it was invisible to the observer-thank god! But why does it continue on inside? Runnings of shivers up and down and close to the surface, he could withstand them. After all, he believed many were like him. He laughed. His psychiatrist already somehow conveyed he was one in a million. Wow! One in a million should be great but he knew it wasn't. He was one of a few. Food? Of course he ate food but it turned into slime, sliding down his insides across the jitters. Drink? Yes, but it was like putting water thru corrugated configurations and it shimmied down his insides like snakes down the sand. What a creepy feeling he would think. I think I will go kill someone again today. Well, maybe I could wait, two today is enough. I watched them die thru my already dead like eyes. I need patience and I have it because the slow chopping of body is uplifting to me. Chop, chop, chop—did I read that in some book? Anyway, it is my method. I like it and refuse to choose another one even the ones I read in novels. I get away with it cause I look just like you—average, kindly enough and never one to be suspected of any butcherous activity. My right arm unites in the life/death chops and my shoulder sings songs of alleluia. Inside I am a bit odd but you'll never know. I pick people just like me, the average American. I have such a deep love for my work as it is rewarding and revitalizing. It doesn't ease my shimmerings inside, I haven't found a way to do that yet. The kills do seem to validate my insides as doing the right thing. I know for sure that I will walk thru life innocently and die a peaceful death cause I blend in so well. I have no motive you can trace, not even in a broader view is there one. So, I will live a long killing life for sure. Lonely, you would think so, but I am not. I go about my business with a delighted heart. My psychiatrist thinks I am the normal neurotic type who comes for therapy. In actuality, his use of words highly interests me, and if I use any pattern, it is the number of times he uses 'un-huh' or 'I see' to determine my kills that day. One day I could not keep up with his words and I thought well maybe I' ll kill you if you are not your regular self in a short while. I laughed and he asked me what provoked my laughter and I said a funny image of a man and woman dancing. Possibly my mother and father-ugh! I only like him for his clarity and precision the way he chop chop chops words with great patience. I know I'm rambling but I am not killing rite now, so I may be less precise. I see myself as a humanitarian contributing to the growth of the population. Killing a woman kills her eggs. Isn't a woman so close to an animal with its eggs? And a man's sperm like a woman's milk flits out. I have never had an ejaculation-I don't know why, I've tried—but stopped twenty years ago. It doesn't interest me. I have seen it in some porn movies and it looked stupid and ignorant and crude. It made me furious too. So I don't do these things that make me furious anymore. I have no anger really even with my doctor it is a feeling of patheticism for him I feel. So I go about my business as any workingman does trying to do a better job next time. I can be critical of myself, true, I mean to kill better every time I do it. I did six kills in one day!! Some were of people no one cared about to even notice they were missing. Runaways, bums, a couple of truck drivers, what a day! I have a lot of money so that is how I pay the psychiatrist. I have a nice SUV, an Explorer. I've walked by you, the reader, on a couple of occasions, and I thought of killing you but for some reason I haven't done it yet. I need to look at you more. There is something about my rhythm of chopping and your pacing or speed or timing that must match. I can't figure it out but it is true something has to mix right. That's why the police can't detect who I am as it is about internal matching rhythms. Please don't think that I am implying you have internal shimmerings-God no! I apologize, as I do not mean that at all. I'm fascinated about me and the way I've looked. I think it has to do-and this is vulgar-with the rhythm of a man's testicles and a woman's breasts as they walk along. Well, no reason to go into it. Oh Honey!! I had the weirdest dream last night!! Ha! ha! I can see you are thinking it was about a man who was dreaming and that its true don't you think? Let me ask you, did I just wake up or am I really this way? Go slow here now, you were believing me weren't you now. Well, its true. I was dreaming and I just awoke and called my wife to tell her the dream. I've been watching you watching me. How does it make you feel? My wife soothed me and calmed me by saying nice supportive words. She has no tits no legs and no arms. What a mystery she is to me-you too? Now I've got you a little messed up, that was my intent from the beginning. I've not succeeded yet. I'll probably just kill you chop—your end.

The Electrician

The electrician feared electric shocks. They would go to his very heart and sting him in thousands. It only happened a few times to him until he found a new use for them. It wasn't totally innovative and thus he felt uncreative with it but enjoyed watching the process and the results, results that were often surprising yet always the same. It was a long time that he was here now and probably the best thing for him, as he did have a 'side'—his mother's words meaningfully and forcefully given to him. He had adjusted, as only one can, or at least he resigned himself to this place. So what that I electrocuted nine people-they deserved it-everyone of them, my mom first, then my dad who would take me fishing and my older brother who taught me baseball too. I get him to go into the small room in my cellar. It has open dangling live wires that with a switch I could turn them on and they would drop off the ceiling like fishing net and wrap the person in a frying pan of screams and burning flesh. That took care of my Mickey Mantle brother. I won't go into it but burying him was very difficult. My mom, my first, was easy as she is older and slower. I convinced her to try on a waterproof vest kayakers use to see if she liked it. I went behind her and quickly plugged in the electric cord into my makeshift but extremely efficient wired device in the vest and watched her, and close to what I imagined, I am happy to say, she began to dance and dance like a puppet on a string to music inaudibly playing an Irish jig. What merriment and just plain old fun I had with her! My dad was special. He was a strong man still, even now in his sixties. So I had to factor in that piece. Having to slightly hurt him before electrocuting him made me feel a bit like a coward but I brushed it off because the end result would be the same anyway. I was in fact a little bored about having to kill my dad but work is work. Every Saturday morning he would take a bath even if he were going to sweat and dirty himself during the day with some outside work. On occasion, as a much younger person, I would walk in accidentally-why didn't he lock the fucking door! So going in would not be a problem. I had to make sure the radio was on and nearby, and that I could get to the hairdryer too. What to hit him with was my major concern—I just wanted to daze him to be sure he couldn't get out of the tub. A hammer was easiest to carry but too likely to knock him out or worse, put a hole in his head. So I pondered and pondered on this piece and I had to be sure my brother was not around as well. My mother, the first, was found in the river a few weeks ago, poor thing I cried a little as I am in a mourning period for my mom. The police said it was a drowning by accident and that was that. We buried her with care and lots of love too. Well anyway, one Saturday morning I knew my brother was to be out and my father to be in the tub. Still perplexed as to what to hit him with, I reluctantly decided on the small stool in the bathroom. I would just have to tell him I needed some fatherly advice and go to sit on the stool but grab it and hit him on the head-remember, remember—not too hard. I had practiced hitting a tree and then some cats to determine just the right force to stun and not make go unconscious. I felt really good about myself as I think I knew it precisely though I had not been using a stool. We'll see I thought. I sure hope I do it right. I should have thought about the little stool before but I was kind of locked into the idea of carrying something in from the outside. Oh well, unthinking me! When the eventful morning came and I walked into the bathroom and asked dad if he could help me out with a girl friend problem I was having, I actually sat there for about five minutes and he gave me good advice too. He seemed so unconcerned about his nakedness and I was not bothered either as this time I was glad that he had not locked the door. Gracefully and with good though not exceptional speed, I reached down, took the stool in my right hand—the one I had an operation on a long time ago-and swung it in an up, up and over motion and down onto his head. Lucky me he had his eyes closed-something in no way I could foretell but did appreciate. I got enough of his head to get him dazed as I had wished. Guessing the weight of the stool on its downward flight was a work of immediate determining, but I got it right. So, now that he was dazed, I quickly as I had rehearsed it, threw the radio in and grabbed the hairdryer and threw it into the bathtub too. It took me about five seconds—a longer time would not have been good. Next, I watched and it was great! Suicide to join his wife and the mother of his boys was the word. Why would my dad do that? What about us sons? My aunt, the one I liked the most I electrocuted next. I just went to her house as I usually did once a month and wired her bed from underneath in such a way that when she changed it, she would hold onto a ball of live wire. I remember people actually referred to her after as a 'live wire'. I had not made the connection. It took a few months to set it up and this one was to be clearly described as a murder-a who done it! I had no fun or joy or anything good in this one! I'll only tell one more as you have enough of a sense of me as to why I am here being caught after the ninth one. What a long boring trial-not electrifying if you know what I mean. I had taken a big risk on number five and also on number six. I then went conservative for seven and eight. Number nine was where I got sloppy. In fact it was right outside this building I now call home. I electrocuted my partner with the wires that were blown down from a windstorm next to the neurological complex. I was hasty, inconsiderate of my need for time and a plan and protection so I would not get caught but I was pissed and lost all perspective. I just pushed him into the wires and was seen doing it by a security officer, and a nurse attendant, and a groundskeeper. Why did I lose my cool? We were talking about the patients and one was my former doctor, who my partner kept calling a whacky quacky. I happened to admire him very much, and circumstances different, I would have liked to befriend him and I had it planned. So I got uncool and finished him off and then went what the hell, I told them I did the others too.

The Director of the Complex . . .

A death today, naturally. The Director of the complex was a very patient man, knew his staff and their capabilities and worked them respectfully and well. Not too out of the ordinary, a death was handled well by the staff and the funeral parlor in town. As always, the director would have to investigate exactly what happened. He was a big man with an eagle shaped head, but no one commented about it in front of him, as word had it, that he had beaten the hell out of some kids as a youth. He had come from a similar position in a different state and was hired because of his strong record with this desperate population. He was fifty years old, and single, with no marriage or children behind him. There were questions as to who his friends might be but it wasn't clear whom or how many he had. Little did they know that he had a fulfilling inner life after work. He had all kinds of fantasies and imaginings and listened to music quite a bit. Having been brought up by a mother and a grandmother, he perhaps had enough of women. He was a loner but social when he had to be for an interview or a talk or some such thing. He came from his mind not his heart, reason being that at age twenty-three his soulmate died in a horrible car accident. The driver was negligent and not paying attention to the road and the maintenance of the car. He had noticed at the gas station that the rear tire was low and needed air but he figured to wait till the next fill up. The tire blew out at sixty miles an hour and the car swerved in the back to the right kissing the guard rail and then careening to the right to side over the white line then back again into a tree where the explosion then happened. The girl, frantically undoing her seat belt was in shock, hands catching on fire, smoke filling the cabin, a stillness of time and space. Finally free but on fire the girl reached for the torrid door handle. Already heart and soul dead, but something in the body of flames that were slowly carnivoring her from the outside in, she kept pushing the door open with cake arms and falling slowly over like a roasted mass, she totally died. She had been talking about her upcoming marriage and her dreams of children and home and was at least able to make two signs of the cross and the beginning of a prayer albeit screaming it out. The Director was the driver. Like a rejected Spanish lover who goes off to become a maid in Paris—as she is considered no good any more-he decided he could not get close again. He feared if he did whoever the woman was would die or that he would and he did not want to experience that pain again. The Director was thrown out of the car with little but a bump on the head. Quickly he ran around the other side of the car to help his love and froze as he watched her burn to death screaming some inaudible words, perhaps I love you? He fell to the ground and vomited all over himself and then lay there looking at the sky-how blue, how sunny a day, what nice pretty clouds—for twenty minutes before another car came careening along and called on the police. The picture seared into his mind of his girlfriend was Technicolor wide screen and magnified twenty times. He wanted to go with her into the great unknown but his body didn't want it. I'll never meet anyone like you ever again and I will never try is what he also thought, never again, I promise. There are four chambers of the heart and three of them died that day. One chamber to change oxygen into blood and gases that's all the heart I need. I can go in my mind but never into my heart again.

The Escapee . . .

Fuck you you bastards he heard the voices say as he slowly squeezed past the drainpipe. Get the fuck out of here mantraed in his head which was different from the usual kill the Pope message. I hate this dirt on my clothes it will destroy me before I get out of here. Finally thru the last challenge, I can stand up though carefully as it is evening but shadows may talk. Where do I go? I don't know anything but the inside for fifteen years Where am I? I will follow the lights in that direction See, I'm walking along I am normal. I did not drown any one or two or three. You got the wrong man! Fire, fire, burning bright what makes the town aglow tonite? I like water and fire but not mixed together! Let me see here, a street, a good one for walking. I like the lights and the way the fresh air that breezes on me. Get the fuck out of here! That voice again. I can see a young couple walking, and I need his clothing but it is risky with her there too. Oh there is a man coming up the other side of the street ahead of me. I'll get his clothing, actually he is more my size. I just have to whack him real hard on the head. I will have to use my hands. Oh well, now I jump out at him and whack him and he goes to the ground and rolls to his feet, fists clenched. Oh shit! I hear as I go towards him and smash into my jaw goes his fist and I fall to the ground, this is crazy! He goes to kick me but I grab his leg and kick up into his balls and he screams a man's scream going towards the sidewalk I aim another kick but I miss him. He plunges his fist into my stomach but I hardened before he got me. I kick again as he gets up and this time I catch him in the ass and he goes sprawling into the street. Fucking bastard I'll kill you says the voice in my head. I go towards him and all of a sudden I am hit from behind on my neck from some other guy whose wife and child have begun running away and yelling for the police. The guy from behind comes closer to grab me and I swing my elbow into his throat and he falls flat croaking by my side. The guy in the street is getting up slowly but I better get the hell out of here. I begin to run in the same direction as the woman and the boy and as I catch up I see them turning, thinking, "Papa," I body slam the gal into the bushes and I grab the boy for a bargaining chip. He struggles and yells but he is light and I run away with him. Police sirens or maybe there is a fire! As the police pull up to the kerb, I run towards a darkened house and bash the door open with my shoulder-it may be my house for all I know..I've got a gun I yell and I'll kill the kid! That stops them. I planned on killing the kid anyway but now I have an excuse. In this dark living room I can slowly adjust my eyes and feet better. I slapped the kid so hard on the door jam on the way in I must have knocked him out. Come out with your hands up!! Oh God that sentence again Fuck you! You bastards I retort. I see a red dot come onto my shirt and I drop to the floor wishing I had a gun. Stay outta here I warn with fierceness. I actually sound crazy. The boy ! Where is he?! I get up to go where he was and I am suddenly smacked towards the left direction by a candlestick held by the boy's hand. I fall and I am exhausted and I try to get up and the boy runs to the front door screaming I got him! I got him! He is out the door and in come the cops. My hand goes up and I hear a blast of the gun and a bullet goes right thru my forearm while I slowly rage at them as they grab me I fight the fight of my life wounded and all. I throw two aside then one aside I am finding new energy in my raging flailing defense I hear this loud wood hitting wood sound as the billiclub smacks down on my head and I enter a deep sleep. Upon awakening, I realize I am sore all over and home and tied down. I could have killed the Pope but I will wait till next time. Last nite I think I killed an altar boy.

The Killer . . .

His tool bag is heavy but it has all he needs to work. Not the best of jobs, full of danger, but financially rewarding. As he gets to his appointed spot, he lays out his instruments carefully and one at a time. No need to rush or messy things up. Looking thru the binoculars he sees his paunchy target at the starboard side of the boat. Unlike what people say, he will know what hit him. He will know that a bullet entered his chest to be followed by an insurance one. He will know because he expects it to come. I told him I would get him and I told him about ten years ago. I like to have my people think about living and dying for some time as you can see. From what I understand, he moved from one country to the other every couple of years in total dread and panic. Pill popping and all kinds of medicines kept him just off the edge of the deepest fear pit but never to relax at all. So, finally here I am in my boots and jeans. I prefer to call them dungherees and a nice plaid shirt laying on a knoll overlooking this little harbor town. I hate—and this is honest, to throw out every outfit I wear to work, but that is part of my job. I am normal and I have two wonderful children who want to become doctors. I can afford to send them to med school easily. My wife works as a social worker with the poor in the inner city. She is very generous with her time too. I of course am a traveling salesman though actually my real job is for the CIA in Washington. It dos not pay enough and when I learned in training to be a crack shot, I found other ways to make a buck. For instance, this job will pay me 100,000 dollars and the time it will take about 10 hours of my time, about ten hours twelve years ago and the rest now. I use the Internet at work so I don't consider those hours to be going to this job, though maybe I should. Here in this remote village of Cadaques, north of Barcelona, I reconnected to my target. Working for the CIA I can find anyone pretty easily. It takes about ten minutes to find anyone except for the most secretive, and those who never wish to see anyone they know again. So, I kept tabs on him over the years and just feel now in my heart that it is the killing time. Why him? What had he done ten years ago? He killed and raped two sisters ten years ago, two young kids of a single mom who contacted me through a mercenary magazine. I also waited ten years to see if he would have children but I guess my info to him scared him from that. To get me to work for you is a ten stage process as I do not want to be known for this part time work. First you contact my post office box in Denver, Colorado. You next must follow the instructions from Vancouver B. C. The instructions say to go to the Miami International airport where you leave a note for me in a certain stall in a certain men' s room or if you are a female, at the bottom of the # 5 best seller book at Barnes and Noble there. The note you leave me there tells me all you need and want me to do. Then if I decide to take in your project, I get from you a 20,000-dollar deposit and the deal goes on from there or not. I am an honest man and have never kept the money and not followed through. If you give me this down payment, you then must fly to Rome and be third person on three consecutive days to get off the bus that stops at the Porte di Pronzo at the Vatican. Then I see you and you do not see me. I require this precision of my self as well and I need the perfect protection. Now I have the money and the photos of who you are so, next I direct you through another series of clearings to the point where I have that information necessary to fully do my job. We never meet. I do my job. I cannot reveal the steps necessary to make our contract, as it must be kept a secret. To the boat again and my man. I have a silencer and a beautiful weapon. To hold it is an ecstasy few know. I have carefully and totally surveyed my shooting ground in the rain, heat and cool, so I guess you can say I am thorough. Next, I raise my rifle to meet the dawning day as my target moves to sit himself at the side of the boat. Coffee, bloody coffee!

The Priest

The priest had devoted his life to the mentally ill at the complex. Middle aged, handsome and tempted by many women, he held to his celibacy vows. He had hopelessly fallen in love with Jesus as a young boy. He didn't know why or how to explain it. It was a mystical love of sorts; one he felt matched his very essence and journey. His love of people was immense and deep especially these poor people with whom he worked. He felt Jesus in the hearts of all and often felt moved by his flock more—more by the ill ones than the healthy ones—at church on Sunday. He didn't understand that but it was so. The priest had been a chaplain in the Vietnam War where he was wounded in the stomach by a hand grenade. He had lost so much blood that the doctors used the word miracle referring to his recovery. The priest did not know he was injured that bad so involved was he in caring for the other soldiers. When he realized, it he asked God to let him live on a bit longer till the other men were safe and getting the medical help they needed. He remembered his blood mixing into his greens and a bluing effect emerging. He kept on praying and administering the sacrament even during his own pain. Working here at the complex, he was used to seeing blood and hearing the screams of the insane ones like in a jungle or battlefield of death. Why do I love my work was a question he would ask once in awhile. He never could answer it though, he just loved it is all. One of his favorite patients was Dr. Joe, the former surgeon in town. He never knew him well but he found him to be very sweet when not being violent. The priest wished he could cure all of them but particularly Joe, as the doctor was known to be good but not well known as a person. Let me have another miracle he would think. I think Jesus is healing the doctor the best he can. On his rounds the priest would touch those who allowed it and he sometimes felt an energy pass thru him—a spiritual flow that sometimes moved him too. One time, however, almost in an exorcism way, one of the patients was restored to complete mental health after the priest asked for it. The man was liberated from the chains of mental disturbance and began to talk coherently such that two months later he left and took up his old way of living in the town. Word got out and the priest was more sought after than before, being seen as the healer that he was. He had also another healing that was considered unbelievable too when a young boy had been hit by a car and broke his lower leg. It seems that the priest held the boy's lower leg and it mended almost immediately. The priest wished this would happen more often and knew it was Jesus' work and that he was only the vessel. The townspeople felt a great love for him and wanted him to be who he was pure, guileless and a Son of God. The priest would never tell anyone of the visits he would experience. Jesus came to him several times over the year. One time while vacationing in Spain on the Costa Brava in a town called Tossa de Mar. Jesus met him. The priest had hiked up a small mountain across the cove at the edge of the village that had a matching mountain on the other side of the inlet about three hundred yards away. The sea would wash up between the two onto the apron of the little town Boats would dot the area, fishing being the way of the townsfolk, and a bit of tourism. While on top of the little mountain, the priest stood to rest and looking out over the sea, a movement on the twin mountain caught his eye. It was a little beam of light that began to move slowly off the land and arch rainbow style up into the sky coming towards the mountain where stood the priest The golden light—round in shape—became bigger and bigger and began to descend to where he stood. The ball of light landed about thirty feet away from the priest and began to slowly move towards him at ground level. The light had a circumference of about eight feet and the priest could see that an angel was carrying it weightlessly from behind. As this ball of golden translucent energy came towards him, he noticed that it enveloped him and the angel. The angel came right up to the priest and then; amazingly, he turned around immediately in front of the priest and took one step backward and entered into the priest's body still shimmering with light. As the priest absorbed this energy he alternately felt like the angel and himself. Next, on the other mountain, he saw Jesus and Jesus began to take the same air path of the angel rising into the sky and arching over and descending onto the mountain where the priest where the priest was and Jesus stood a ways from him and then began to walk to the priest and then embraced him and said Go and heal my children for you are my brother, friend, and soul. The priest hadn't known he was weeping gently and felt so humble and blessed and empowered and he agreed to his task and bowed deeply to Jesus and the request. No one was in the area to see this event which made it easier for the priest to have to explain what he saw and what happened. But this day he rededicated himself to his work with an even deeper love than before knowing that Jesus was with him in body and soul. Some sensitive townsfolk where the priest lived often felt an aura around him but they thought they were crazy for thinking such thoughts and kept it to themselves and secretly enjoyed it.

The Hotel Maid . . .

She was about 25 years old, French and pretty. You would think that she could do some modeling but no. She is a maid here in a hotel in the town. Her blond hair was always tied up in the back so she was free to see where she may go next with duster and cleaners. She was paid a bit more than minimum wage but she was at least happy to have a job in the town. Besides, she accidentally came upon a way to make extra income. One morning as she was cleaning room 16, door open, she and the room a little messy, the man from room 18 said to her that she did not need to clean his room today. 'Ok", she said and went about her business. About 5 minutes later as she went from the room towards the bathroom she saw him standing in the doorway to his hotel room. In awkwardness she did not know what to say and continued to the bathroom. "Hi." Says he. "Did you change your mind about your room she queried?" "No," he said, "there is no need this morning." Next he made a peculiar gesture with his right palm showing some dollar bills and passing the money into his other hand. Then into his pocket. She looked at him and he smiled back. Suddenly she thought of what he was suggesting. Nothing was said but she felt herself to be correct. He wanted to pay me to have sex with him. How bold and daring! I am insulted and angry! I continue into the bathroom. "200 dollars," I hear him say. That is a lot of money I think to myself. Am I thinking of doing it with him! Yes, I think so because I could use the money. Well, maybe I am making up the whole thing. I remember the time I went to buy bread and the guy handed me back the change by gently holding my hand under his and putting the coins into my palm. I immediately thought that he wanted sex with me but all he was doing was giving me the change. This time is different as I am sure he said 200 dollars and it is interesting. I said,"ok" and then proceeded to jump out of my skin to where I do not know. My heart was pounding. Did I really say yes? Does he have a condom? I am not sleeping with him without a condom. Yes, he has one he acknowledges. So, I close the door behind him and take off my rubber gloves and move toward the bed. He is not bad looking I slowly remove my tee shirt and that is all I have for a top then I take off my bra 34 b small, firm, and perky. He takes off his top and he is a hard bodied guy. A little like my boyfriend. I ask for the money and he gives me the 200 dollars. I slowly become embarrassed. I conitnued undressing. If this were strip poker I would lose in 5 hands. He slips down his jeans and the silent theme in the air is Mr. Goodbar. I hope he comes off quickly as my job is to move to the next room. I have not been checked on by my boss in several months. He goes and just as I felt and heard the key in the lock, I know I was to be fired and also knew what my next job would be

The Therapist . . .

The Therapist had often been traumatized as a child. He saw the weaknesses in his parents and tried too fill in the empty energy with his own boy energy. Boy energy that fills in for the parents' holes is called blind love. The boy would do anything for them even though they were abusive. He did it and therefore it was predictable that he would become a therapist in his life if not one of the other helping professions. He did not know that he was to become a therapist and in fact began his life in a different career. He actually was a schoolteacher to whom many teens would come to tell their problems. He would be flustered about what to say so he would send the teens to the school counselor. One day the school counselor suggested that the teacher become counselor, and then he would know what to say. Not a bad idea was what the teacher thought. So the following semester startup, the teacher was enrolled in the first course of a counseling program though not sure he would go further with the courses. The fist class, called Sensitivity Training-what could that be all about anyway—was a question on his mind. He attended the first class and to his astonishment the professor put the chairs in a circle then made some opening remarks then fell silent for the remainder of the night. What the Hell!! What the fuck is this he thought! Everything everyone began to say was stupid sounding. Let's tell our names and where we work, let's tell how old we are and what we hope to get out of the course, etc. Why did it sound so hollow? What had the professor done? He merely said nothing and that is what he did until he said class is over. At one point towards the end of the class, one man got very angry and yelled at the professor and said if he were not going to teach he wasn't staying and in fact never came back to class. This yelling seemed to spark interest in the group and everyone came awake, some fearful, some angry too some sad but all involved. The young teacher thought I love/hate this and I may/may not come back. As the next class day approached, the excitement, anxiety curiosity and interest all brought him into class that night. The teacher who had a beard because he did not want to bother to shave was the only bearded one in class. Another man quite older, challenged the teacher to shave and show his real self/ totally stunned and as if he had an axe go down the middle of his body to cut him into two, the teacher broke down crying, and openly vulnerable. In such pain, and oddly, gratitude, the teacher then told some of his personal story and all listened attentatively and he could not believe that they would give him their time and attention so that his heart could be healed. On review later that night, the teacher decided that he wanted to know more of himself and of others and decided to become a school counselor which led him to become a therapist. It was a long journey, as he had to learn method, theory, and technique. He dove into his past and the current therapies learning about his self and how to implement them in private sessions and in clinics where he did internships. At one hospital where an innovative psychiatrist was developing a model of comprehensive care including physical, emotional, spiritual, interpersonal, and cognitive methods the teacher fell in love with his life's work-and he became very successful. Dedicated to his own therapy and training, he became skillful and very perceptive. He had come to the neurological complex some ten years ago from some other hospital but he wanted to live in small town and not in a big city. He had a modest apartment where he hosted several small parties a year, often had people over and found time to be alone there too. He did find the work here more challenging than at any other hospital. There were the criminally insane who intrigued him as well as those who had lost their minds. Of all the patients, he was most drawn to Dr. Joe probably because the doctor resembled his brother. The therapist would carefully observe Joe hoping to find a path into his mind from where he could lead him out. At times he thought he saw a way but it was more hope than reality. After many days and hours of observation the therapist decided to mirror Dr.Joe in his movements and sound makings. He bought a pair of slippers into Joe's room and then began to imitate Joe's moves-so delicate, so fine. In his mirroring he found a certain peace within himself and wondered if Joe was experiencing the same peace. The therapist thought that after twenty minutes of intense and minute following of the gestures that he might be able to anticipate the next move, make it and then begin to have Joe follow his moves and then try to lead him more and more with the intention of somehow moving him into reality at some point. The therapist did this for two months every day and finally he had to try something else, as Joe was not following him even in the slightest way. The therapist did not know that in fact Joe in that deep psychosis so not understandable was on occasion trying to reach thru the massive stone wall of illusion and despair that he lived behind. Joe would cry a bit, though no tears were produced. The tears fell into his blood internally and the oxygen was his Kleenex and his wastebasket was his lymph nodes. How can the therapist not see me? What he does see is a kind shell, an immovable rigidity sometimes a catatonic entity. Hopeless except for his God who somehow stands inside behind him, Dr.Joe lives on. Why doesn't god talk to the therapist and tell him the way to help me out? A rage now develops in Joe one which he does not choose and slowly dissolves him into his own blood system and does not know what happens next. The therapist, immune to the helplessness of his work, will try other ways to get to Joe. He decides to try family therapy but none of the family members can be found and word has it that they are all crazy and could not help much anyway. The therapist knew that the drugs were helpful/harmful but anything less was impossible Even knowing the impossibilities, improbability and terrible success rate with these kinds of patients, the therapist refused to surrender or give up. His open optimism even helped other staff members. His love of his fellow man was deep, broad, and intense he would continue on treating the patients the best way he could with the best resources available to him at the Complex.

The Visiting Salesman . . .

They hoisted their glasses in a toast to me. How bizarre, but I raise my glass back to them. Next, surprisingly, they wave to me to come on over. They look like they are in their twenties or early thirties. That must be their second floor home across from my second floor hotel room. Now, I am in my fifties so I am a bit cautious about this possible adventure of unknown. If I were in my twenties, I would be down the hotel stairs in a gulp. Now I realize that they also can see me when I'm in bed very clearly. Well, no thank you, I wave them off and close the curtains. This is a strange little town but it is a quaint hotel and I love the way the trees hang over the streets-seems so ancient that horse drawn carriages should be the means of travel. Only two nights here and then I am back to my wife and family. If not for business, I'd never come back-creeps me out! Now, my second night, and the same opening act, a glass raised, a wave and this time an ok from me, what the heck. I had had a few drinks already and sort of to myself hoped this would happen. The drinks make a yes appear from behind a wiser no. So up the steps to their apartment and the door opens as I arrive at the top step and I am welcomed by this young couple, an attractive young couple. As our awkward at first conversation develops, I come to know that they are living off trusts and need not work. Often they make friends with the people who stay in the second floor hotel room across the street. We have some more drinks and all of a sudden I feel the beginnings, unwarned, of passing out. The couple says things are fine and not to worry but I fight against it as I have never passed out. Slowly it dawns on me that I have been drugged! I struggle, and struggle against the growing loss of consciousness. This is a painful battle, what do they think they are doing? I'll call the police upon awakening, they know it. Oh God, maybe I am not to awaken again! A fear races thru me with a power, force and drive! I'm going to be dead in minutes and these are the last people I will see?? Don't give in, God please help me!! Someone! God, the Father Almighty, Creator of Heaven and Earth . . .

The Director and the Florist

The Director of the complex felt his penis enlarge and contract as if its own knowledge was only half loyal to him and how he'd lived his life. He masturbated for the first time in years and he was thinking of the florist in town. The thoughts of her made him produce even more milk-like substance just after petite mort, petite mort, petite mort! On the bed, having let go of years of pain and loyalty to his first love, he felt free, personally and orgiastically free. Tomorrow he would go buy flowers for his office. He would see and wait for what he felt in her presence. The next day he and she were there. As always, he felt a twinge for her, but today it was more full—genitally full—and desiring. It seemed too soon to be so filled again after last night, but it is so. He loved carnations—the poor man's flower, as it was called—but he felt the presence of angels whenever he had the carnations in his home for several days or more. She came to serve him with her usual aplomb. This time she noticed an extra member in attendance. Could she let him know without embarrassing him or herself? She had no words. He seemed somewhat uncomfortable with her this time, as if he were being pushed to be different from somewhere else.

He did one of the most stupid, idiotic, spontaneous, smart moves he ever made in his life. He put the carnation stem into his mouth and gutterally said, "Toro!" The Florist burst into an open laughter full of sexuality and openness. He laughed also and reddened himself to the degree that he wondered how the hell blood could concentrate in two places so fully. Next he again spontaneously said, "Would you like to go for Spanish food in the nearby city?" She answered "Yes." The first and best response for any woman, she knew. She awkwardly put her hand on his arm when she gave him the flowers. I just wanted to feel him. It was accompanied by anxiety, and this for a woman who was very comfortable with men. What's happening to me!?

A longing for him so absurd this soon, but he has been coming for the last several months to shop. What happened?! Grow up!! I feel like a teen and new again. As he leaves the store I feel like crying with sexual joy and sadness. What is going on? The Director of the complex feels grandly foolish and out of control. What had he dared to suggest??? It was organic orgasmic or orgasmic organic, whatever it was, it felt human and he was on fire. At home with this last thought, he began to cry, a pain filled deep-purple cry—one that comes from the nowhere deep inside of us and yet from the everywhere of our being. Cleansed, purified, and free, now.

Tiny is as tiny goes . . .

Tiny lived in a hotel room on the darker streets of town where the prostitutes, pimps, and downside people lived. He was one of them, small, petty, menial, and nasty too. He had seen what he even referred to as more dark places and people than he was. He would feel a bit higher classed on occasion when he walked on these darker streets where drunks, both men and women, lay around sickened and vomiting from their obligations. He knew in his insides how much better he was as a person because once he had stepped inside a church to get out of the rain so he felt as if he'd been to mass-more than these dark side folks had ever done. He lived alone but would see Janey on occasion for some sex—he was one of many he thought, but he would think he was the only one. Funny how the mind makes one special even when not. Janey was a prostitute and made money to keep herself in clothing and food and a room. He did not know where nor did he care where she lived, as she knew where he lived. His room was small but just enough for Tiny. His brother was in a mental hospital on the outskirts of town-he never saw him but thought of him at times. His brother, Joe, had become a doctor and did well but lost his mind and had become a bad, dangerous, kind of crazy. Tiny wouldn't let that happen to him—having sex, eating food, and walking around a lot would prevent that. Tiny wasn't that good in school like Joe was but that did not matter much. He got his check every month and that was all he needed to get by. He liked languages most of all in school-Spanish and French. He thought of himself as if in Les Miserables, but had forgotten most of his French. He hated Italian-his father was from Italy and Tiny hated his father too. He wondered if his father was a queer. Joe had said that he was, but Joe said a lot of things that Tiny found out not to be true. Maybe though, in this case, he was right. His father was weird working on shoes all day long. Hell! People's feet! What drew him to that? Was his father a shoemaker too? Tiny didn't know much about his grandfather. So, Tiny lived in his four-block area called neighborhood except for his daily ten-mile walk out of it, and he really loved it there. He knew most everyone by what they did but he did not know their names except Janey the prostitute. Big Nose, the milk deliveryman, Bitchy, the landlord. Screwjob, the guy who owned the corner store, SOB, the laundry lady, A-hole the guy across the hall, FU, the cops who drove down the streets, all had names. Once in a party in his mind, Tiny had a ball introducing everyone. A-hole, meet FU, Screwjob, this is SOB. He laughed in his head. Janey, this is Bitchy! But that didn't happen in real life. Oh! The Salvation Army guy—Drunk Ass—nice clothes though. Tiny had gotten a shirt that said Facconnable on the pocket—what the hell did that mean? One said Daniel Cremieux a nice name-how rich, how gay—not in a sexual way though. Tiny had a lot of fun in his mind. It was crowded with people and things to do and places to go. He would go into a picture of the Eiffel Tower he remembered from a French book and would climb up the tower without the police interfering and would walk around Paris for free—no ticket necessary to fly there either.

Silence

He was whistling. Silence. He was whistling. The sign says silence. He could not read or didn't care. Not caring about a sign's statements may not be a grievous offence but somehow this time it seemed so. Where else did not caring occur by this man? Positively overspeeding the limit was one that everyone did not care about. So, not this one but where else? Do not walk on the grass—he didn't care. No jaywalking-he didn't care. No loitering—he didn't care. Was this a man who did not care about anything? His shoes were polished, coat and pants pressed so he did care there. His hair looked good as did his moustache so he cared there too. Oh! Maybe this was a man who cared only about himself! Who else exists except people to get in the way with their signs? He is a sociopath I am thinking, he doesn't need people, he uses them. Anything others say goes threw his I can/cannot use you filter. If you can be used you are at the mercy of his not caring. If you cannot be used you are still at his mercy as you get emotionally and mentally annihilated. What is this man trying to tell us? I am fine? I am damaged? I am alone? It is a puzzle. He seems kind and affable with his not identifiable tune or song he whistles. But he is not. Behind his presenting aura is someone who truly hates. We just get to see the tail end of it as it comes out in not caring. At the front end, inside, he writhes and churns in a hate/rage that is maniacal. As it comes along the path from front end to tail end, it lightens up. But in the beginning there is fury unbridled, scathing rage, humiliation and deadly mortification. Each time he goes along his continuum there is a lessening of the dynamiting murderousness and the horrorific suicidal impulses. So it moves along further until at the tail end it is merely not caring. This man needs his progression to continue uninterrupted because devastation internal and external would occur otherwise. So the momentum continues and this happens to this man ongoingly. Like the pistons in a car, millions of explosions

120

keep him going safely. If all the explosives gathered to go off at one time he would kill or be killed He's crazy but doesn't know it. He lives alone-always has—who would live with a non-caring man? He even talks in a non-caring way—dismissive, off the point, and deflected. His eyes don't look at you. He hardly hears you. He eats out all the time but has no taste, He does not know he does not care. It is invisible to him. He thinks he is ok and just has some bad luck with women. Silence, and he whistles. I was only observing him, little did I know that he was preparing himself to blow his brains out that evening.

Great Bose Headsets . . . !

I piano wired him on the spot. I do not even know who he is. He was wearing those big Bose headphones, so I don't think he heard me and not even his own screamings. Great Bose headset . . . The sky marshal, I had just guessed that there was one on the plane, and the male stewards were upon me. In an airline seat you don't have much to move around in and so I was an easy catch. Putting on the cuffs meant a big change in my life. Prison, maybe execution, I do not know, but life as I knew it was slipping away. I had forgotten how I hated to be made central when I make a mistake but everyone was looking at me and I felt embarrassed. The rest of the flight was filled with" I am glad it wasn't me talk" to "It must have been his hard luck to be the one, and other such worries. Being satisfied by complaining to others they let off the anxiety. One guy looked at me admiringly too. The dead man, oddly enough, to him I begin to feel close. He had been pushing his seat back all the way and I could not move. I had 7 inches in front of me and boom! I went nuts.

The Jamaican . . .

"Yea Mon!", he said as he inhaled his smoke. It added to his fun time besides going to the west end of town. He came to town originally as a waiter working in the local cafe. He'd read about the job in the big city and nearby when he had landed from Jamaica striving to begin his own life anew. He had left home not on the best of terms but . . . Anyway, here in this odd town he felt included. They all were a bit strange. He got the job even though he felt a prejudiced feeling in the interview. He assured the owner his kind were guaranteed hard workers and that seemed to be the winning phrase. His accent had also caught hold of the owner as well. A melodic, yellow bird, kind of sound and rhythym. Getting stoned added a bit to his relaxation and peacefulness that the townsfolk did not know about. In Jamaica he had worked at one of the resorts and they all smoked there. A smoke and a blue mountain was all he needed. Red Stripe on occasion helped out too. How can he replace them here? He made contacts in the city that at least provided 2 out of 3. The beer can be substituted he thought. He had met a Korean girl and some asians and had seen a black man in town but other than that, diversity was scarce. He had a scar on his cheek in such a place as to be attractive. one earned from a knife of a woman at home. This was not the reason he left. He found a small studio near the West End and that suited him and one that he did not have to worry about the upkeep. It was in a building where lived one of the girls who worked at the salon above the florist's shop. He would see her in the hallway of the building and in fact was quite attracted to her. Time would tell. If so, he'd like to live with her. It's always best to live with someone. He knew that it was good for the health and the fun. She always smiled at him and as she passed him by.

The Plumber

Underground with the rats! What a job! Well, someone's got to do it and why not this plumber? Where is that broken pipe? He found it dangling like a steel girder as if launched from the darkness behind. He flashed his light around and saw the nested rats reluctantly leave home. His knees ached in tune with some waltz pace. Can't stand up and dance here he thought. Oh the dance and her, that sexy one from downtown moved her body like a combination belly dancer hula girl. Who could resist? He knew for sure that his knees were not aching then nor would they that night. She laughed when he told her he was a plumber and suggestively played with the metaphors that were easily available. He had trouble maintaining himself as she was alluring for sure. Well, where is the break in the pipe, the source? Crawling more towards his broken target he found his mind wandering to the barroom and the dance gain. I better not waltz thru this job or fox trot either-it is one that the complex depends on getting fixed quickly and well. It's wintertime. Now at the source he concentrates on his task. It is not as bad as he thought, so he could daydream a little. She moved to him when waltz time came, some old Beatles song, some beautiful one. In unison they moved and not in haste, and the blending occurred on the body level. Did she fall asleep in the dance-impossible-but he thought she did. This pipe is like my pipe, rigid, hard and carrying life sustenance. Almost done with this piece he moved to the next part of the job. He laughed in his mind when he thought of all the similarities to the pipes and human bodies, what they do and how they look. Suddenly he heard a scream from the first floor above. It was more than he expected. It sounded like a wounded enraged animal, actually blood curdling. Maybe all the screaming cracked and dislocated the pipe! He had known some of the residents before they went berserk. He knew the electrician and thought he was a pretty level headed guy but ya never know. He knew the doctor and the orderly. When he worked on the toilets above, he could see them but they were not there, at least he couldn't see whom he knew. One inmate seemed fascinated with water and a story was floating around about him drowning several people in fits of madness. The plumber most liked the electrician; for god's sake he used to work with him on the other side of this wall though just for a short time. The plumber felt bad for the young man who lost his family but unbelievably-he was the one who killed them. People are strange. You would not think it of him. Well, dancing again underground with that woman so sweet, so alive, so new. She took him to her apartment and treated him to a geisha mistress rape experience. That he'd not forget. When he left he realized he had not asked her name or number all night and she did not offer. He did not have the courage to go back and knock on her door to ask for that. The plumber had been married to a black woman and was never well received, but because of it as he was one of the native townspeople, he got some respect. One time he got drunk and tried to make love to his wife's sister and that was the end of the marriage. His ego needed stroking from the newest places, otherwise he felt a bit low. Gathering his sexual self together he decided to go to the girl's apartment-it had been two weeks now. He walked—you can walk almost anywhere in the town—down the street where her apartment was and he upped the stairs two at a time-more anxiety than excitement. He knocked on the door and drew his breath in fully exhaling deeply three times to get more control of himself he knocked again—no bell and he heard some sounds inside like puppy yelps or breath filled sounds but no answer. He stood there and began to wonder what to do next. He thought to call out but what would he say? All of a sudden the door opened and he saw her and she said come in with some enthusiasm and he did. He can't report what he saw as he is inside now.

The Murdering Wife . . .

Slowly and surely she pushed him off of her. Dead from a knife through the heart. At first she thought that she missed because he made some moves as if to recover. Life with its dreary try at more. She had known him four weeks and the time had been fun though—truly internal to her—she thought he was a jerk, but a jerk with money. So a fast wedding and a fast death-so many rituals in life. She would leave him here and go underground for six or eight months. She had places all over the world, She was a loner as if she had created every letter of the word. She would get ready to go back to Detroit, her least favorite city but the most black in America. She, being African American, would fit in that city just fine. She looked like most blacks like most Asians look like Asians. Once when she visited Bordeaux, France. She was invited into one of the homes that were built inside the walls of the old stone and rock buildings. She immediately bought one. Hers had a wine cellar with a hidden door to the back of the house and street. This, if she could recall well, was after her 3rd husband's death-poor guy. She learned French pretty well and kept up at the local brasserie to practice French.

Killing me softly . . .

Quietly, without much fanfare he took the pills that killed him. Just moments before, he did a few last minute adjustments to his will and insurance policies knowing now that they would not be paid as originally promised. Choice less, only one to be made, he did it. He had planned it for quite sometime, as he did not want to go on this way in life paralyzed by his neurological disorder. Needing help for everything was not how he would let it be. He remembered Wickie his Lhasa apso and how kindly the vet had let him die-why not this for humans too? Dr. Jack Kevorkian needed more support and if he had received it it might be his way today. Choosing this day was easy too as it was his birthday, his last one He wanted French vanilla ice cream fed to him as it was his mother's favorite. He also wanted some pablum as he had grown used to it these days anyway. The convincing of the person to help him do it was difficult for both him and her, but she was strong-always had been-and she did not want him suffering either. She said she would do it knowing she would be alone after it. If the doctors found out there would be hell to pay. She would be secure financially as they had planned for that. She was no longer working anymore except on her arts and crafts about which she became internationally known. She was an elderly woman and the law may not even prosecute if they found out. It is rumored that doctors give patients extra morphine to let them go sooner rather than stay in great pain As he did not want to go to the neurological complex on the outskirts of town, he was not offered that possibility. Besides he had worked there as a younger man and the noises he heard there were unnerving to him continuously. He promised himself that he would never end up there. He had worked at the complex as a researcher, gathering data on the comings and goings of the patients. He only stayed there one year before moving onto the job he retired from three years ago. He was not happy with retirement, as he loved his work. He had spent 37 years doing it and he missed it still. His children, all grown up, were sad to see him in this condition. So, all are now relieved as he has stepped through that veil to the other side. When its time to cross that silent sea, who will sing for me . . .

Whasssssup!!

Whasssssup!, he yelled, tho he did not want to know really. He learned it from his father who yelled all the time. Yelled at him, his sister his mother, his neighbor. It did not matter whom. His father was an orderly at the local hospital and had to yell at the patients a lot. He worked at a mental hospital and had developed a yelling habit that now he couldn't prevent. So the son caught on too and yelled too. The father appeared angry most of the time—he attributed it to his work environment. He had promise as a young man but was in a car accident and had slight brain damage but unfortunately in the area of the brain that deals with analytical skills. His going to college was over, everyone knew it. Besides, being black didn't help either in this mostly small white town. That ongoing consciousness was almost debilitating, certainly maddening. He found a job at the hospital and to his surprise found a girl who liked, married, and gave him children. He had to work mostly in the wing for the criminally insane. It was dangerous work but he was always strong and very quick. Whenever the patients got wild, he would use the restraints moves very well so no one got hurt. He helped restrain Dr. Joe when he first came in. He did not understand why his own MD was so out of control. He had always been so kind in the office visits. But now, having to restrain the doctor, was strange and awkward and he felt weird about doing it. That was awhile ago and even tho the doctor doesn't recognize the orderly, the latter pretends he does and even feels like a patient around him. He had seen the doctor for common ailments and even once for minor surgery in the office as he felt close to the doctor although the doctor always seemed professional and less of a person if you know what I mean. Now the roles were reversed to a certain degree the doctor is the patient and the orderly is the caretaker. The orderly, after a time, was the only one who could take the silk slippers away from the doctor at nighttime. Maybe because he was recognized or just threatening because of his strength, the doctor would make low growling dog like sounds when first approached, but in time he quieted and allowed them to be taken away for the bedtime. To protect them, the orderly always put them into an old shoebox every night. The orderly was proud to be the only one who could do it for the doctor. On weekends the slippers stayed on all the time. The orderly was a happy man too, losing his abilities and knowing it and being black were angry making ideas to him, but he made a life for himself in spite of and to some disbelief of others.

The Staff at the Neurological Complex on the Outskirts of Town

That doctor, or at least former doctor, now patient, is strange, no one comes to visit him, and we are sure he was kind to people and served them well. He mentions the name 'Ed' on occasion but it is embedded in a mélange of stilted sentences so it may be just a fractured phrase. By that we mean 'ed' at the end of a word like in shred'ed or at the beginning of a word like 'ed'ify. We really do not know. The doctor, Joe is his name, we heard that he had something to do with shoemaking in addition to doctoring. There is evidence of some homosexuality or sexual contact with his father who from the rumors we hear was a sexually troubled man. Joe in a locked room with bars on the windows. He wears whites and slippers that is all, all the time. He fiddles with his slippers incessantly as if trying to repair them in some way. We notice he uses his hands in motions that would not occur when putting on slippers. We think or let's say we know him to be paranoid schizophrenic with outbursts of rage and fury, unpredictable, and unnerving, as he is our most dangerous patient. We wonder what goes on in his mind, we medicate him, not all of us in agreement, in the type, kind, and dosage. That is one of our problems. To watch him finger the threadlike thin silk fine lines on his slipper and his fascination and slowly bobheading as if suspended somewhere above his neck, is pathetic and warming. What meaning or understanding he finds in the slippers-those of a madman's world—where it makes common sense like the dreamer in the dream, it makes sense but not to the awakened one. We had given him shoes originally but he used them as weapons against the food dispensers. Can a mad man have foot fetishes? We don't know for sure or not. With the slippers, he didn't throw them but cradled them in his hands like tender broken birds. His charts don't help us much and truth be known, we probably have given up on him, his being lost and all. He has no response to us—not visual, auditory, or kinesthetic, except his outbursts. We are not good on knowing what other internal things might be happening like some arthritic or some other physiological problem. So we let him go on till his body dies. We think it a cruelty. Internally we fear for ourselves as we are doctors too. Joseph, named maybe after St. Joseph? He is Italian, probably catholic. We don't know if he was suffering from those inhibitions so powerfully inflicted onto the very vulnerable young children of catholic schoolings. St. Joseph, the as if father of Jesus, became very background when his Son came into his own. Did he go insane when that happened? Is Joe following some pattern after his possible namesake? We have tried all the medical, psychological, neurological approaches so we find ourselves wandering into alternate thinkings. So must we go on? Yes, we do. Is there a light at the end of the tunnel for Joe? No, there is not. His spirit has already been crumbled. We think he is possessed by Satan or demonic forces that have overtaken him and now he belongs to the darkest world of all.

The Lying, Shaming Nun . . .

Colorless not flat no, not, not, not not. Ok kids after doing square dancing we will all try to jump over the wastebasket—with a blindfold on our eyes. Excitement flooded the room as all the kids wanted to do it. And thought they could. . One boy became anxious fearful thinking that he could not do it and imagined himself falling and making a fool of himself so when it became his turn he refused to do it because he knew he couldn't do it. Blindfolded. The leader said," ok Stand over there with those that did do it. The boy moved to the side of the room where all the kids were standing. They had all had succesfully jumped over the pail. When the next person to jump came into the room a bit uneasy but greed to put on the blindfold. When the kid was put into place the nun removed the pail and of course the boy did not know or see this. Next he jumped—he probably would have fallen into the pail and gotten hurt the nun immediately replaced The anxious boy now realized that he could have done it and he felt deep shame that the did not try. He then thought of the deceit of the trick and became angry. Should he tell the others or not what was this lesson to be? Trust and you will succeed not knowing that you were actually duped and helped. Not did o it and to see the trick being created in front t of you and then shaming your elf/. It was a game of shame. You thought you did it but you didn't really but when you get to see the next you know you really did not. When you see what really happened while approaching the pail. You are not as good as you think you are. The boy wondered if he could have jumped it. One kid demanded that he have another chance and he did it successfully and blindfolded how did he feel did he reverse his shame?

The Japanese Girl . . .

They met at the hotel coffee shop to talk bout some real estate business. He had in fact fallen in love with her. She did not know this. He wanted to tell her in some way but he could not figure out how to pull it off. She was Japanese and stunningly beautiful with all of the features in the most perfect places and a body to die for. Her winning personality and smile of ginger love invited all to say hello. She was now a teacher having studied art at the university. There were rumors of her sitting for some of the artists in town and that they could not capture her but for some of her body. The word was that many of the artists had sex with their models but she supposedly never did. Gossip . . ." So now that that is done may I tell you something on a more personal level? I am very attracted to you and my being 58 . . . I hope you are not insulted by my saying it to you." "On the contrary, I have fallen in love with you too, but my being 28 I feared it would turn you off as I am probably as old as one of your daughters." He felt stunned, grateful, lucky and a little crazy and relieved. She looked the same at his reaction." I love the grown person in you, age does not matter. They looked at each other with tender souls and hearts of open gladness. He pulled her towards him in a possessive way. She felt safe and protected by this older man. not a father figure but an older man. She had always been drawn to older guys. Her brother was ten years older than she and she looked up to him and her father in warm, admiring ways. "Will you come to my place now?" she asked. A "Yes arose in two places. He was surprised at his response but pleased too. He picked up his sport coat, took her by the arm and walked off. He knew where he was going

The Head Nurse . . .

I'm so lucky that I do not have to deal with those looney criminal jerks!! I like my new position of dealing with the nurses only, and my set nine to five pm hours. It lets me have my nights to myself, well at least my husband and me. He's not the greatest, but I have a lover on the side and between the two of them I have a complete life. My husband is a good guy, a bit self centered, catholic, and therefore troubled sexually. Hence, my lover with whom I am totally sexually uninhibited-a total female animal presence. I cannot say his name as you may know him from town. But back to my gaggle of nurses whom I freely boss around and delegate practically all of my work. It leaves time for me to read mystery books and other novels of interest to me. I don't trust one nurse in particular, a Korean girl. She gets her work done but always looks overtired in the morning when she leaves. Another nurse who lives in town and who hardly speaks to anyone does great work anyhow. I was brought up by my father and his partner. Dad, after Mom died in a boating accident, came out of the closet. This happened when I was five years old and it was just the two of us for three years. There was a woman who also took care of me but she has since died too. I loved her. But Dad got his man that year and he slowly moved into our house. I liked and grew to love him and he was kind of the mother to me as my father's role did not change much. It was ackward when I said I had two Dads to my friends and I soon learned it better to just say one. The other kids knew I didn't have a woman and female mother and assumed one of the men was like a mother I guess. Later I went thru some cruel times as I was called faggot, queer, lesbian and other names I won't say here. In high school I became pretty much a loner and read a lot. I rebelled against my Dads ferociously and had them in a quandary many times. Drugs and alcohol and lots of sex became a way of life for me. A loner and lots of sex-who cared at all! No one. I was an object of affection you could say. In college I read Buber's I—Thou but I related more to I-It and still fear the former mode even today. Funny to think that I work with people that are really its! At least to me they are anyway. I see some of the doctors trying to talk in the I-Thou but the patients can't understand any mode of communication with them. Yes, occasionally I have taken some drugs from the complex and had a good time with my boyfriend. I know how to count pills to not get caught. And some of those nurses that steal the drugs! Actually two are in Nurses for Nurses hoping to get dispensing privileges back. Sometimes, on the weekends, I go off somewhere alone for a day or weekend trip. My Dads have moved to a gay friendly city and are doing real well. It is thirty years that they have been together now. Me and my husband have fifteen years and I am in the best time of my life right now.

Some Walking to do . . .

Wooden, slow moving and kind of weighted down
A man walks slowly toward his town
He will arrive because he goes in that direction
Still his heart moves in despairing pumps
Oh to be light and quick and free
This just isn't what life is for me
Carrying along the generations of repression
How to resolve it? Another confession?
Can you accept your very existence
Or do you go on in some form of resistance?
Who knows of all this in your being
Only those with the gift of seeing
Well just in these moments I wonder
What pressures life has put me under
As I get closer to my town
I feel lighter because I'm not its clown

Just Up . . .

Just up now a little while to go for coffee or make it here is my choice. The dog is asleep, at least I think so and I'm half asleep too. Well, maybe I'll make the coffee here. No dreams to write down or none that I recall. It is painful to write as I do not think the muse is kicking in rite now. I guess it is like everything—practice counts. Oh I remember a dream! I will tell you from the woman in the dream—her perspective. She was yummying it up with sounds of pleasure as I'm sure it was her 25th time that evening how sweet of her—how paid of her too. How many men she must take care of in one evening. Me, I'm one. I live alone in a condo in town where no one can hide except in the bathroom and there it may even be possible to be alone. Alone in one's insides in one's thoughts and image making machine where all is private unless one wants to be made otherwise. There, in a naked way, one is what one is inside. How much passes from the communicator to the outside is depending on the environment I suppose or who the receiver is. But there is the quiet bathroom of one's mind—one can let in whoever one wants and be safe unless one is a maniacal lunatic then even what comes in by choice can turn to be out of control and a case of madness like what happened to Joe. What a sick dream I'm thinking and I hope I have more quite similar

A Delay

A delay? How come? Something in the pilot's window pane-go to gate 12. 159 people's stories changed. Mine was simple or at least I aimed it that way. My father had died last evening and I was to go home. Home and my father, two difficult studies. Home was not where the heart was. He was an alcoholic and rode it to his death. Locked up in that pail of alcohol swirling around on his insides all alone. Not available and not wanting to be with his eyes still on his ancestral and birth home. What did he leave behind that he never carried over? What secrets, debts, obligations, even loves he left on that old earth? I don't know. Maybe under the alcohol was a good human being, maybe even a loving one, surely a hurt one. How many people surrounded him there that he had to leave and with courage to do so. Well there was nothing there anyway for him to make a living. Heart broken, soul lame, mind weakened and body drunk, he made his way here with his despised mother and lonely, homely, sister. He became a fireman and married a woman from nearby in home. He would feel delight-he rarely allowed it-in his new position and country. But soon the old despair and longing came back. Ugly again, haunted again. Well here's the drunk thank god. Well, thank no one, it was totally out of control, it had him big time. Ok now kids couldn't be helped was natural and he was proud, but what skills did he have in that area? None so let them suffer a same living, after all, he did. So that is what me and my brothers did. We took on his pain and tried to heal him and damaged ourselves in the process Luckily we recovered-different times you know. So re-routed onto the next hopefully, we'll get there well. Home, an Irish home, is cool, damp, religiously strong, psychologically weak, and with an Irish mother. Faded dreams impregnated gleefully/regretfully and surely in sin, well, it was what it was, it lifted the despair a bit. Her complaint and addiction was him. She loved him, probably idolized him and strongly knew it—didn't know it. She didn't want to know that she later punished and excluded him. Ok, no more dancing, no more partying, no more sexing—maybe for kids—but was that just an idea to hide her cravings-she was beautiful. His drinking really took off but he was in that much pain and terror. My brother identified more with my mother than I did he and he developed her punish/exclude tactic after a while. I stopped going near him. I think he also felt my father's terror. I was first born and king so I escaped the worst of it of it. My relationship ended with dad when I was 16 years old and we never talked again-very much the cutoff, the exclusion, the annihilation. Well, I could go on but flying now—delay over—I can think of the funeral. My brothers will be there, and my Irish mother-sister-daughter. What lies there in wait on the ground? Go into it in peace. Find resting peace and I will fly into you tomorrow.

And so it is . . .

Laughing and its neighbor crying will soon stop. They will soon stop forever. My existence, this 230 pound space I take will become vacant and I will be invisible. I won't be able to make sounds, movements, nothing. Death will come from the ground up into my body. It will take my feet, ankles, and lower legs, and, my hips, my walking legs. It will take my upper leg too. Next my genitals and hip area will go. No more sex, no more hip pain. Slowly it will go up my back taking the life out of my intestines leaving what last meal I do not know. Moving to my lungs and heart-did I really use my heart well or was it undeveloped in some ways? Broken a few times and maybe dead before this unchangeable forever takes me it may have been a premature death—one in life. Dying of an unrepaired heart, but showing everyone else the opposite truth. My lungs automatically doing their job slowing down to my last exhale. My mouth, thru which I have sent ugly sounds and good ones too. Did I say the good things enough times or now do I say one last one. My nose, did I stop to smell the roses? My eyes, did I see enough and my brain, brain dead, did I use it well enough? Did I use only the famous fifteen percent? So death finishes me thoroughly. Now where am I? I'm on the other side of the veil between life and death. I am near to the veil as I am a newly dead one. When I look behind me I see millions of other dead ones, all gone before me. Oh such sweet escape . . .

Birds Talk To Me . . .

   She was demented, a slow growing dementia but she felt happiness believing that the birds talked to her. She reported receiving spiritual guidance, emotional support, and creative ideas. One bird told her she was Mary Magdalene cleansed and wedded to Jesus She believed it in her heart and prompted herself to spend many hours in front of the Monstrance, the home of Jesus in her special church. She would not try to convert people to her religion though admired those who did evangelize. Some birds were her support emotionally as they represented joy and peace in flight. These birds told her of visions far off where she could not see, of Holy Lands full of angels and grace abounding. She imagined that the birds said such sentences as "We hold you in high esteem, we see you as precious, and we cherish you deeply." And she felt her spirit soar. On the mental level the birds told her she was creative and able to do anything she wished. Quilting, stamping, knitting, beading, photography, just to mention a few. She had tried some of these pastimes and did have a starting talent though not many knew of it. Sometimes she would fly with the birds but she could not imagine what they saw all the time and this she attributed to her sense of respect for the feathered friends. On occasion a golden eagle would fly high up overhead just out of her vision yet the Golden Eagle saw her and felt a great love for her for her love of the birds that talked to her. Believe it or not the Golden Eagle would also communicate with the woman-amazingly—thru felines living with her. The woman did not know that not all the time were the cats speaking to her just for themselves. There were only special—and I cannot tell you—the things that were said to her. The woman, unknown to her, had become named 'the walking animal lady' to the town residents. She could be seen walking at 5:00 in the morning and chatting with the animals easily. In fact, some observers felt sure that this woman was some sort of animal goddess mother waking up her charges for the day ahead. The only relative known about in this ladies life was a loving and loved in return sister who lived in a group home in town. Here it is also known that the lady was like a guardian spirit sent to the home. Maybe she wasn't suffering from dementia-townsfolk-out of fears can be descriptive in some hard ways, especially in this town where the neurological complex is . . .

The Psychiatrist . . .

Graceful, classy, with a subtle style, he had won the hearts of them all. Yes, there were some complainers and critics but none with malicious intent. In his speaking, he was clear. In his teaching, he was precise. In his leadership, he was a benevolent authority. Well read in many areas besides medicine, he encouraged his staff to develop a taste for it-some did and were glad, others didn't. He elucidated very complex ideas into understandings that his people could know and implement. He was of German ancestry. His father had been in the SS in Berlin first, and then later was sent to France where he climbed up in rank to lieutenant colonel. His father was a fierce believer in the Third Reich and adopted all of its beliefs and had met Hitler many times and he claimed them as his best moments in the service. He had ordered the murders of hundreds of people and at one time as a sergeant personally entered a French village and went into several houses and killed all the inhabitants. He felt he was doing the right thing-killing Jews and the enemy. The psychiatrist loved his father very much and it was not till long after his father died did he find out the whole story. He was shocked as he had grown up with a man who ran a small veterinary hospital near Berlin and called him Daddy. This dark story of his father's doings and not knowing it but the energy or ideas of it being there made a mystery that drew the young boy into studying mysteries and what greater mystery than the human mind. His father had said yes of course he was in the war, all the men were and that it was terrible for them and it is in the past and that is that. Wars over, we lost, what is done is done; closed book is what the father said. In some way though, the horror was passed on to the child's mind and he reacted to it. The psychiatrist spent years in therapy. Coming to understand his father and his family. He had found the right profession for himself and he continually loves it. His favorite patient was Dr. Joe whom he had met at a couple of CME workshops. He found him to be down to earth, natural, but a bit aloof at times and with a good sense of humor, but that was before Joe came to the hospital. The psychiatrist carefully read the notes daily written up on the doctor. He was particularly interested because of the meetings and the brotherhood. He could see no progress in the doctor since day one except the adjustment to hospital life. He decided to follow his care daily to keep himself sharp and out of love for Joe. He followed Dr. Joe's care for months and nothing was different. What must have happened that afternoon in his office the psychiatrist wondered? Psychotic breaks can be personally devastating but they also can be treated and lived with. What kind of break was this? Did they check for chemicals in the room that he may have mistakenly taken? This began way before the end, and was there any signs? The psychiatrist had unanswered questions. He wondered through controlled way he felt that he did. Controlled meaning he had ego strength to deal with it. He knew he could murder someone but wouldn't, he knew he could blow up a house but wouldn't . Perhaps if the doctor had had therapy, he might have curtailed those inner coercive energies that work in and against us all. The psychiatrist's mother, an Austrian, was a strict disciplinarian, somewhat a furher of her own over her little army of 3 boys and a girl. The psychiatrist felt her love nevertheless, and that generation didn't verbalize in that way but showed you their love in their behavior towards you, he quietly remembered. Well, he had worked and studied hard, married a great woman, and fathered three wonderful intelligent athletic boys whom he adored. He loved spending time with them and was happy he did not have to do much disciplining as his wife took care of that.—kind of like home he would think. His wife was a doctor too but suspended her work to bring up the boys. Later she would go back to work. They often went into the city for cultural events and socializing, as the town in those areas was flat. He enjoyed his family, staff and job here in this town

What got me here . . .

Struggling along thru several attempts to express myself in my twenties thru writing, I found a book whose title I do not recall . . . the book though gave me hope that one day I could put into words some of my despair, despair of the robbing kind, of the draining kind. That word again to describe that mood is so elusive I cannot hope to retrieve it. Think damn it! What word was it? Moving along in a fractured path of real how can I bless the smallish tokens I have without the pity of illusional freedom? Control your self for a minute, an eternity even, so that 'no' emerges in physical ills and emotional upsets and exclusions of love in pain and anger-good you've got it now so well done to tell someone! Choose a 'yes' freedom one that frees me from the downs of inhibition and stop sign living. Go forward into the unknown or at least follow it easily feeling the anxiety of its unfolding-but it is safe. It is all on a paper on a notebook that withers and dies in some sort of neurological complex on the outskirts of town. I hate this!

Other Thoughts & Things

A Neurological Complex on
the Outskirts of Town . . .

Who lives there in that strange place? I hear they jump out of windows onto the concrete. What kind of mysterious force and knowledge of one's own mixes to direct destruction? These people fascinate me! I am one of them, or am I? I do not know what I need to duplicate their lunge. The visitors to the Complex are sometimes indistinguishable from the residents. I visit there in my fantasy-I am too frightened of the insane to actually go there.

Now there are stories of those who go in and come out alive, or at least walking. They do live till they die in other parts of town in other probably buildings surrounded by concrete.

What is deep in the complex that heals? This I don't know. Still there is something that kick-starts a life again there. How fortunate. I guess, some would say not so fortunate, to go on again. Maybe some profound spiritual movements occur to carry life on.

Joseph, a resident there, is a friend of mine. He is now crazy, beautiful, and non-functioning. I don't go to see him-remember I fear those kinds of people. He lived downtown and perhaps the gases of any downtown made him lose his mind. I don't know but there you have him in the best place he can be oddly enough as I view it as the worst. What happens and what they do in there, I wonder and fear.

Don't tell me! Hey I am only writing this on request it has nothing to do with me! I really don't know what I'm saying—a little like Joe.

A Small Pad

He has a small pad but it fits him just right. He can do what he wants where he wants. It really does not confine him as some said it might, in fact he feels a certain freedom with it. Keep it forever he thought, well maybe yes and maybe no, he would have to see. He viewed it as it is what it is for now. Maybe with more money, he might get a better one but he was very frugal even down to the smallest item. It gave him time to decide. He felt no confinement in the space but actually a certain freedom determined by the limited space itself. A creativity could emerge that otherwise might not. The containment created liberty in a certain way.

A Theft . . .

Opportunities for learning come in strange garb. How could an incident that inspired such fear and outrage be the prelude to a dramatic life style change? I was robbed! As unbelievable as it was—living in a second story apartment—I was robbed! Anger, hurt, resentment all flooded my experience. What timing! My brand new stereo equipment had just arrived from a PX in the Far East—made possible through a best friend doing a tour of duty in "peaceful" Vietnam. The fury gradually morphed into anxiety. Even with the best of my possessions now gone, would he, they, come back for a second go through?

My general feeling of security was now replaced with uncertainty, raw fear. Even though it was eleven o'clock and time to go to bed for the night, I'm frozen. Calls to my friends, looking for support, had just increased the feelings of dread—"if they got in through your second floor porch, man, you're not safe at all!" That didn't help! "Do you have an alarm system?" Duh! I thought I was impregnable! "Do I own 'protection'?"

Who me? You mean a gun, right, not a condom? No! Oh, wait! I have a baseball bat, left over from some long-ago sport phase. That's what I'll take to bed with me—protection! It didn't help. I didn't sleep much that night.

This was my Thursday night—the Thursday before the weekend workshop at the Boston Gestalt Institute Training Program. This weekend was different than others, a special guest was coming, Dr. Joseph Zinker, from Cleveland. If he was as good as the trainers painted him to be, maybe he'd help me—they'd talked about him as if he was magic. Maybe he would know where I could find my stereo.

Still a bit disoriented with a lingering sense of paranoia, I drove to Boston. Driving in Boston is an experience that generates paranoia and exacerbates exponentially any dis-ease associated with traffic, Kamakasi-style drivers,

151

and grid lock. For a time, attending to avoiding potential crashes, drove my night-before-trauma into the background.

Finally at the workshop site, I got inside the room where people were into contact and honesty, openness and forthrightness, and anger. I wondered how might this help me now. So, we sit on the carpet in a circle and this mystical, soft spoken accent laden, slim Dr. Zinker says "what is bothering you?" Me? I wondered why he was talking to me. Could he tell I imagine he is my thief and he's feeling guilty about it? "Nothing." I state firmly, dishonestly. He says to me, "You look frightened. Do you want to tell me about your fear?" Contact, and he sees me and that helps me see and experience me too. A trembling, a loosening begins to occur and he doesn't seem so frightening, but rather compassionate, warm, peaceful and supportive. I begin to tell him my fear story.

He suggests that I lay on the floor as I had remembered myself in bed on that scary late evening. Take my feared position and show everyone? I hesitated and then decided to try it out. As I lay there pretending to be in my bed, I started to quiver like I had since the incident but, somehow, simultaneously I felt a bit of safety in my surroundings now. "What are you feeling now?" asked Joseph. "Fearful, anxious, angry, confused and suspicious," I reported " . . . and sad . . ." How alive in all these feelings, I felt! What he asked me to do next as an impossible challenge. "Stand and become the intruder/thief standing over yourself in this bed."

"No!" I stated. "Impossible! I hate whoever it was who stole from me."

But again in that soft supportive voice he said, "I know this is difficult and lean into the standing intruder."

My body wants to get up and become the intruder and I realize it and follow my movements, trusting the process, almost watching myself from within another place. As I emerged into the intruder's space and stood over myself in the bed, I felt a rush of adrenalin, power, and intensity. My mind flooded with awareness and memories and new insights into my own intrusiveness and intimidating aspects. I don't remember all the words I'd spoken then in that session, but I do remember the intensity of feeling, the oceanic rush of my self and my body as I synthesized these two polarized parts of my self, the victim and the perpetrator. Tears filled my eyes. Rage filled me. Deep personal satisfaction and gratitude filled me. To Joseph I looked and blended into his warmth and support, love and guidance. As I felt myself coming out of my work, I felt respected, seen, heard, and held by all in attendance. Moving to the background, I felt a solidarity, peace, and self confidence I had not known. Joseph went on to work with others. My fear was gone as was my anxiety and dread.

When I returned home that Sunday, two young teens approached me and told me where I could find my stereo. That night I lay in bed listening to beautiful music that played outside of me, inside of me, and in between.

Thank you Joseph Zinker, I will always remember.

At The Well . . .

I am standing by the well and Jesus and the woman are having a dialogue about from where He came and to where He was going. He looked to be in the prime of his life, about 32 or 33 years of age. He had a glowing energy about Him so he must be a special man. He looked at me and I felt this rush of love come from Him. It surprised me a bit. He asked me, "For whom are you looking?" I said, "For You." He smiled and said, "What can I do for you?" I said, "I feel like I probably will not go to heaven but to hell." He said," Do you want a drink of water?" I took it because it distracted me from my kind of crazy statement. "Let this water purify your soul in every way." I felt stunned and entranced with the beauty of my feeling. I felt a deep movement in myself, one of great healing. The woman, though not supposed to be speaking to Jesus said, "My, you look different after taking the water." I thanked her and Jesus again. Then, I decided I would follow him wherever. "Where do you come from," I asked. "From my Father in Heaven and I am here to change the history of the world, to save as many people as I am able." I wondered about His lineage and I asked Him, "Are you human?" He said, "I am the most human and the most divine in my heart and most human in my body"

Bob West . . .

Bob West, a young GI, came home on an uneasy Sunday. How could he know it would be a curious welcome? At the gates of his parent's home his dismay began. Bucks, his loving little dog, did not come running to meet him and this was not a good sign. If anyone were to die he would prefer it to be the dog and not one of his parents. He had shucked corn and pulled beans from their hidden wombs and did all the things a little bit well a small farm was producing. Growing vegetables rather than livestock was his family's forte. He was not married but did have his first sexual experience at age 16. Bess the girl from the small town up the road. He really loved her deeply and there was no using or manipulating in the relationship. But Bess was a student and Bob was not. For this reason they parted ways not without a ritual ending and a lot of tears. Bob was a military man, thought he'd stay in more than 20 years or more but a tragedy would befall him in his future. Bob would lose a leg in a motorcycle accident some ten years from now. It could not be saved even given what modern medicine could do. He grew wonderfully up until that time then he became very morose. Near the stairs to his parents home lay Bucks, old and tired, and flapping his tail on the ground to the tune "Gonna find her . . ." His parents came out onto the porch to greet him and they looked in good shape. Bob sat down and had a mini stroke that he recovered from, but he had to leave the military.

Can the Heart see . . . ?

My heart pounding with pain each beat. When is the last one, who can know? What realities that I have disturbed and that have disturbed me now course through this heart?

The time when the man in the elevator pulled the gun on me, heartbeat.

The time I had my first sex, heartbeat, the time of my first love, heartbeat, many more. But the biggest heartbeat of all came with her and all that she meant to me. My heart, genitals, and mind and soul all beat to the same rhythm of her, her movements, her inhales and exhales and her words like individual geniuses coming into play each time uttered and of course only at the best time. You little fool, you young fool, you old fool each time it can be said but what about the heartbeat as it goes along? It surely is not a fool. Why the ache, what am I to know how to understand it . . . and the longing, for what, for her? It reaches into my cells and beats on its own. Paradise is the fool and we succumb to its lure and then carry the label for paradise-fool. But one cannot be a fool and not love long and yearn and then he is civilized—I suppose and is accepted by all the dead, masked, beings that live on here. Then lie on your deathbed wishing you had done differently you fool!

Fretting the Guitar . . .

Frustration is what it is. Why do I continue to do it? I say it is to keep myself humble and learning but I don't get anywhere with it in reality. So, why not let it go? Because I still love it. I have had a guitar since I was 16 when I bought my first one. No support for it but nevertheless I tried. I took some lessons and didn't get too far. I essentially am a beginner's beginner—very Zen! I do go to it still trying to create a rythmic sound and beat and still come away frustrated. I go to it automatically and most often come away feeling like I had not accomplished anything. Sometimes I take it up and put it down after one minute cause I can tell where it is going. I must have over a thousand dollars of CD's, tapes and books to play from—it looks like a pretty good professional library too. Fingerpick, flatpick or strum, which defeat do I need today? Why not mix them all in and feel totally frustrated again! Me and music—I love it! I don't go to any shows or let's say ten in my life because I hate the crowds. I love to listen to music, mostly folk, bluegrass and the oldies but I don't feel myself deeply in it. I wonder if I get dissociated from it because of the anger my father said thinking the note was to him. It said, "Well tuned tonight, what do you think, Frances?" He was in a rage about it thinking I was criticizing him but it was not the case. If I look at it from his point of view I would have to say that he did not see the guitar case at all. He must have been drunk for sure as it was right on the dining room table. So, there my father was accused by his son of his entrenched and entangling sin. Guitar and me cursed in one moment forever? Possibly. Perhaps just plain lack of ability can account for it too.

From Dog to Mule . . .

Madison is awake. What joy, what work! This ever present demanding little being! How sweet he is and what a handful. Black, white, red, and brown, what a delightful mix of color, shape, and form consummating in this bundle named Madison. The only thing we'll take out of the town that we didn't like was its name. What a neighborhood that was—snobs, snobs, and even dogs were snobs—such petty little people. Turf was every summer How did we not know and get off the way we began? Well, some unaware/aware arrogance and pride and do you know who I am attitude on my part—just like them. I am so tuned in to the environment that I piled it up—as usual. Want to know what is going on? Check with Radar Ed. It is in the air (field) for anyone sensitive enough to grab at it. Actually, you must let it come to you; grabbing at it makes it disappear quickly and not be available for you. One must wait and only sense what is there to be sensed. Clairsensient is what I am—to energies partially emotional energies. Clairvoyant I am not always had weak eyes—not like Francis with the ant on the stick. Clairaudient—I have some of that too, but not very well developed cause I can hear well what is not said but I can't hear it before it is said. Oh well, Francis the Talking Mule like a football player—what a sad youth but what a recovery! He made it though the exclusion . . . . Cost him a lot. His mother attached and his father detached were too much strain in his blood system and it was a leukemia that finally took him out of this realm of life and into the reaches of the otherland He must be proud of his creations—the kids they seem all a bit ideal and not down to earth. Why truly deeply no grandfathers for them to see and know? His new pledge to never see him again lasted thirty years to death.

One Officer and One Gentleman . . .

He smiled, an Aryan, sparkly-toothed smile. Hovering above were shy blue eyes but cold intent ones. He knew what he was to do, its a job. On the train gently rocky riding along sat his American target. A nice blue suit and red speckled tie—clean. This American was an assassin but now was to receive his own medicine. The German officer had his hand on his gun a not uncommon pose for him. He is closer to the American man now who is sitting in a chair alone in one compartment. The German slowly took out his pistol and shot it into the American's heart. Dead as dead can be. The German went up to be sure that the person was dead. He felt the blow into his stomach as the American's knife pumped a second and third time. The American was wearing a bulletproof vest, as was his custom on the job. Moving slowly from the German's body, the American realized that he would have to jump from the train. He knew that the waterway was up ahead and decided he'd go there. He was proud of himself for always allowing extra time for his work. Who would have figured this as a surprise and a plan?

Oops! He Is Awake . . .

Madison is awake. What joy, what work! This ever present demanding little being! How sweet he is and what a handful. Black white, red and brown, what a delightful mix of color, shape, and form consummating in this bundle named Madison. The only thing we'll take out of the town that we didn't like was its name. What a neighborhood that was—snobs, snobs, and even dogs were snobs—such petty little people. Turf was every summer fought over. How did we not know and get off the way we began? Well, some unaware/aware arrogance and pride and 'do you know who I am' attitude on my part—just like them. I am so tuned in to the environment that I piled it up—as usual. Want to know what is going on? Check with Radar Ed. It is in the air (field) for anyone sensitive enough to grab at it. Actually, you must let it come to you; grabbing at it makes it disappear quickly and not be available for you. One must wait and only sense what is there to be sensed. Clairsensient is what I am—to energies partially emotional energies. Clairvoyant I am not always had weak eyes—not like Francis with the aunt or the stick. Clairaudient—I have some of that too, but not very well developed cause I can hear well what is not said but I can't hear it before it is said. Oh well, Francis the Talking Mule like a football player—what a sad youth but what a recovery! He made it though the exclusion. Cost him a lot. His mother attached and his father detached were too much strain in his blood system and caught a leukemia that finally took him from his realm of life and into the reaches of the earth He must be proud of his creations—the kids they seem all a bit ideal and not down to earth. Why truly deeply no grandfathers for them to see and know? His new pledge to never see him again lasted thirty years to death.

Paris After Dark . . .

In the bathroom at 3:00 am in the morning
As Paris is yet to be dawning
I dreamt myself to awakenedness
And here I do sit in the silence
Time has not been so friendly
Coursing along very slowly
Sleep disturbed every evening
No easy settling down
Just waiting to be homeward bound In granite and plastic
To return to the bed in a moment
To sleep till I wake later
I can't see what else I can do but
Return to the bed from the loo

Paris . . .

Paris, the Seine, the whole place again filled with such glory and splendor. How beautiful you are. Walking your lovely streets, the veins of your body, breathing your Seine filled air, your lungs, seeing your monuments and sights, your vision, and hearing your bustle and noise, your ears. Why yours? Only because you are an alive vital throbbing presence pulsating your energy through the world. Anyone who knows, knows you. You romantic, you! You surprise, you! How sweet you are in your haughty ways. How rich you are in your simple ways. How complex you are in your labyrinthine ways. How you grow and contract from day into night, and again and again. You soar in your opened winged spread flying like a master ship in the sea sky. A journey taken but never to end only to continue on as millions pass from birth to death through you, you will live on indomitably well. Ambulate your passageways and alleys and flower filled nooks and crannies smelling fresh flowers and fruits of the morning's blessings. Caress your Parisian soul though some of you are not even French, and catch a glimpse of your depth and beauty. Look into Paris eyes and see the past, present, and future, all simultaneously wrapped into one. Let your history unfold before us as we come to learn about you who existed before us and will exist after us. Let me touch your heart and soul and know the joy of loving you.

Reluctant Growth . . .

Trickling down, untethered tears
Flushing out the fading fears
Growth coming, going, gone
Pleased to grieve and to mourn
A great change now to make me see
A charge inside from which I grew
Wonderful to be so new, so new
But where to go from here to there
And how to go without my fear?

On Honoring Bad News . . .

Stunned! I'm stopped right in my tracks!
The footsteps I used to make aren't found
Forever now glued here to the ground
So heavy is this paralyzing news
To change my thoughts and my views
And now to listen to different cues
Just to make the smallest moves
Will be a challenge for me now
And sweat and worry fill my brow
And Death to you I dare to say
Now you re not too far away

She wants . . .

She exerted herself just enough to put him over the top. Why the fuck should I do any more she thought. First, he did not deserve it and second a good woman stays one sexual step behind though any one of them in reality is twenty sexual steps ahead. She had felt flirty earlier in the evening and wanted some hot flesh on her so she went to the nearby tavern and sat at the bar where she knew someone would approach her. She was good looking in a Mercedes kind of way. She would lift her chest when she idly would button up a loose one, unpretentiously. The man came over and sat on the stool next to her and asked if he could buy the next drink for her. She said yes and had a standing policy with the bartender to weaken every drink a man bought for her. He was from a nearby city staying in town for business tomorrow. He sold farm tractor parts, a productive but dying field. After a few drinks he said he had to go to his room and would she like to spend some playtime with him. She said yes and they walked toward the fifteen-unit motel down the street. Room seven, he was lucky tonight. Once in the room he approached her and she him in that primal beginning of the sexes to drag release from each other. He observed she had no fear or at least appeared that way. He felt his penis anxiety in him again. Worrying would not help but he seemed to stay erect and he was happy about that. She ski sloped her tongue down the front of his body to his main presentation. She took him into her mouth and swirled, leaped, and thundered around his member. He moaned in deep surprise and pleasure and almost a bit of pain-all new-she was amazing! He hoped she would not mind if he did not return the oral favor as he was inhibited about it. She gently nudged him back onto the bed where he lay down and she, like a snake on a tree trunk, began to move up his limbs. Could he stand anymore? Yes, he thought. Now she lay on top of him and put him into her signifying the beginning of the movement to primal release. She rocked him back and forth and suddenly, like the flick of a cigarette ash; her pelvis snapped his penis half way up the shaft. She did it again and he went into a burst of flaming sperm, crazily swimming towards their target. Did she have an orgasm he wondered? She looked more open and relaxed. She lay on top of him and seemed to have a heat rising from her and his steam intermingled with her. He was totally happy in this embrace. She felt good and slowly relaxed and he felt her slide into an orgasm of long pleasurable duration like a wave at low tide trying to reach the high tide line. Exactly what she wanted tonight. After a while she rose from him and stood beside the bed, dressed and went home. He felt as if he were a woman left, abandoned and used.

She was . . .

She was aware of her body and liked it some of the time and some of the time not, a very woman kind of thing. Those shoulders so broad and strong like a man's this part of her body she disliked all the time. She had to wear a certain kind of clothing shaped to take away some of the width. Oh, she knew it hardly mattered to anyone but her. She never had complaints from any of the men she would meet at the motels. Being older than most escorts and call girls though you would not call her that, made it easier to get men of respect for customers. Having had two children also made for a less than 20 year old body. Most of her men wanted her special treat the one where he lays on his stomach with his hardness going backward between his legs and her pulling it and wiping off the precum to be able to continue, and doing this for an hour. It made the men feel so drenched and so spent because of the wild orgasm that put them close to animalistic senses. Oftentimes the 'short stay' was not enough for the time spent with her. She left one man so drained of his container of innocence that the manager of the motel thought he was dead when he went to clean the room. She was durable. Given her childhood and having to as much bring up her self she became strong and knew the meaning of men at a young age. Match them step by step and then take over when she won their confidence was her method and the men seemed to enjoy. Presently she looked again into the mirror and this day was one where she loved her whole body too. Tonight's work should be fun.

That evening she was strangled to death by a customer . . .

Some musings . . .

Cicadas, bugs and bees
What on earth can we do with these?
To slap them away
On a hot summer day
To keep them away from our cheese.

Twinkle, twinkle say the glasses
As each person passes gasses
But just all in fun
Said the big grossest one
Let's drink to the old smelly masses

Tick tock goes the clock
Time passes slowly by
Now we must take a stock
And blow our money no reason why

Hoses are not funny things
Tho they often hang in rings
Truth it is they are ugly things
But when in use they act like kings

Some Walking to do . . .

Stand by me . . .

She knew her next words would push them over the brink. It did the last time so it should again. She had only recently discovered her nature, one that had played out now for eight years. She was entangled in it and even with her new knowledge she couldn't stop herself. It was in this rage that she felt her power equal to any man's she would think. The consequences, always bloody and once broken were deliciously I'm alive, red badges of courage and pure beauty. Statements that said, "No one will dominate me at any price." After the sessions he would come to her like a little boy and profusely promising that it would never happen again. They both knew better, and he was not lying either. He was so sweet and in her mind she had to forgive him as a person might, apologizing for the finesse of her winning game. Together in their wounded bathroom they would patch her up nicely and then move to the bedroom for a parallel violent sexual contest and both ending victorious in the man's way and the woman's way. "You fucking wimp bastard pussy!" she yelled. Yes it is working as here he comes and I move forward too, my fists raised, going into battle. Feeling rage and falling to his thunderous blows, I taste my blood and swallow. It fuels me as I kick upward into his balls. He lets out a boyish man yelp as if he were finding them for the first time. I roll to my feet and I kick him in the ass. He turned my way and punched me deeply into the area above my vagina and I fell like a daffodiled petite new tree. He jumped upon me and slapped my face without mercy or shame to hold him in check. I scratched his face as tenaciously and deeply as I could and soon he backed away crying like the beaten pussy victim that he is. Time stood somewhere and in some form but not related to me she thought. She could kick him in the head as she got up but thought about the vegetables turning out overdone. She went and turned them off. Fresh ones for a change as she grimaced. Next they went through the ritual cleansing of each other's

168

body, heart, and soul. The desperate lonely feeling behind her and all of this would slowly amble back into her taking its responsible place. Out of this deepness she would struggle and the physicality of it made her feel wanted and real. Men's violence against women. She laughed, but it hurt her to do so. What about women's violence against men? She knew she was culpable for her part in pushing him over the edge. She always told her girl friends it was him. Why do you stay they always wanted to know. I don't know she would say. But now she was beginning to know that it is better than the lost, only loneliness of before him. That scraping, scratching feeling along her stomach and intestinal walls was just the physical part. The emotional part was one of feeling like existing at the bottom of a vast barrel with no way out. Mentally, she would crush and devastate her value. Through the fights she would feel victorious, vindicated, and vilified. Triumph over desperation is a whole body experience that changes you and she was full and engaged, not alone. It was the ebb and flow of her life and she had no intention of changing it. Like many women she knew, she was devious with her man, subtly controlling him along. She wouldn't admit it even to the friends. Too, she knew she could kick their asses. Women push men's buttons all the time, but no one sees it as they only do it to their husbands and lovers who get close to them. With the undercover verbal waterboarding, men have a rare chance as this is a subtle form of women getting what they want. She knew now exactly how to push him. Tweak, pick, say, tweak pick, say, if he doesn't listen then tweak, pick, say on the way to bloody glory. Her friend who asked her husband about everything question after question after question, driving him up the wall in a frenzy then be angry that he would become distant. After all she was just trying to make conversation. Another friend rejects her husband for sex time and time again and then does not understand why she feels abandoned by him. Another one who refuses to visit her husband's family wonders why she feels his anger that she doesn't understand. Another woman, who hates it when he goes out with the boys, and she accuses him of abandoning her. These seemingly small exchanges over time can create an abuse, be it mental or sexual or physical. These are examples of women abusing men. Men cannot easily complain about this issue to anyone, woman or man. Well she thought she didn't care about the others, she knew what she had, wild, mad, thrilling, and dangerous. I'm alive and caresses and hittings more than anyone I know. He is intense, a great lover, and forgiving. What more could I need?

The Town . . .

The town had the usual stores on Main Street and some side streets. It had some long-standing shops too. The Shoemaker/Cobbler shop, the local and only bakery, the hardware store where you could find almost anything except food, and the grocery store where you could find fresh daily delivered food of all kinds. There were only two or three tradesmen in each field. For example, there were only three plumbers in town and two electricians though there used to be three. Many of the buildings on Main Street kept their original character and charm, as the town voted not to contemporize and modernize all of its storefronts. There was a flower shop, Post Office, and cleaners. Two lawyers served the town and were often on opposing sides to each other. There was one doctor where there used to be three, but one had a mental breakdown and the other left town for a medical university. That left one doctor but often the doctors at the Neurological Complex helped out the townsfolk too. Two gasoline stations and one pizza shop with two drug stores make up a lot of the town's places for work. The Complex was the most helpful in employing the locals and it in some way became dependent, as did the people in their connection to the Complex. The town was off a major highway but because there was a city fifteen miles away, few visitors ever stopped to browse. Outsiders would stop if they had a relative in the Complex in town. For those who did pass thru town they were treated to some remarkable sights. One is the color of the buildings on Main Street. They were earth tones interspersed with the color purple, the color of magic or passion. It was done in a beautiful way, not hideous as one might imagine it to be. Parking in town was perpendicular to the sidewalks, which gave more width to the streets. Flowers and green green grass tetertoterred along the curbstones in a very small town well and cared for beautiful touching way. The sidewalks were wide and had cracks that some made sense not to step in. Inside, all the stores were all kept tidy and colorful and inviting. Of course there were some taverns and bars in town along with one very good restaurant. The 'feel' of the town was mostly one of alertness because of the Complex on the outskirts of town. Sometimes one of the residents there would wander unintentionally, or unintentionally off the grounds and into the town. Actually, it happened quite frequently. Only a couple of times were there a major problem with an escapee who was labeled criminally insane. These incidents never let the residents come back into complete peace or ease. The insane one had to be shot so difficult was his capturing and subduing. It was possible to pass thru town in five minutes driving twenty-five miles an hour as was amply posted. Oddly enough or perhaps not, most of the locals owned sport utility vehicles, probably because of the hills surrounding the town and that it could get real cold in the winters even to pipes bursting. There was a lake that became famous because of some intentional drowning of a woman that occurred there and someone with an ironic view called it The Lady of the Lake and it stuck as a name. Walking in and to town was easily done and by many as it is a small town for sure. But as stated, and you could imagine, it had everything the people needed. All types live there too. Lower class, middle, and the upper class, the latter mostly weekend visitors. The West End of town, where the bars and more unsophisticated people hung out was to be avoided at night. Prostitutes, gamblers, and drinkers, all of them known by the townsfolk, congregated there nightly for trouble making and wild times together. At midtown, you could find more middle of the road folks. Only some snuck into the west end, not many. They were the trades people and shopkeepers. Not totally, but a bit so, were the people on the east end of town in that they were more closely linked work wise to the Complex. Many had also been in the Complex for a time, and feeling connected to it did not move to far from it upon release. Perhaps this closeness permitted them not to go back. There is an overall charm to the town, but the people do not enhance it given their overriding mood. The street names were typical, and interestingly enough, no street was named after anyone famous. Off Main Street, there were garden lanes where all the neighbors, though not close, would contribute to the beauty of the walkways and paths. Gaslight like street lamps gave the town a warm glow and invited evening walks, which many people did. There was one Catholic Church, one Episcopal Church, and no synagogues or mosques, though, in the city, fifteen miles away, those services were available. The local priest was considered to be saintly and the whole town loved him. The Representative Town Meeting was a form of political

meeting and governing that the town had since its inception in the early
1800's. There was one elementary, one middle, and one high school all very
small and all the kids walked to their schools. They were considered good
schools though most did not go on to university as there were jobs and money
to be made right here. The town had one famous athlete who went to the
Olympics in 1984 and that was quite an emotional high for all the folks.
There had been one tragedy that happened in the town about fifteen years
ago. It was a fire in the grocery store that is connected to the Women's Clothing
center and the local pharmacy. The fire raged intensely until the nearby cities
fire trucks arrived. The town's volunteer fire squad could not handle the
immensity of the fire. Five people and two dogs died, as there were apartments
above the stores. People talked of arson as they would in this town but nothing
ever proved to be so. It took the lives of the towns only accountant whose
office was in his apartment and this created a financial Internal Revenue
Service disaster for all. It took about five years to get everything in order again.
The owner of the hardware store and his dog, a Lhasa Apso, died. That evening
too, a woman, her husband, and a niece who was visiting also perished. It
truly put the town into a despairing mood for several years afterwards.
Recovery came slowly and rebuilding took time but the townsfolk felt
complete when the restoration was done. A small plaque, in honor of those
who died, was mounted on the new building entrance and it was decided
that anyone who had a similar fate anywhere in the town would have their
name on this plaque. It still remains the same to this day. The town's cemetery
was well kept and pleasing to the eye. Only locals who were born in the town
could be buried there, as it was small. One of the most beautiful scenes was
to look down the main street of town and see the oak tree canopy above. This
also went down many of the side lanes too. It provided for a cool walk and
a more dry walk when raining. The Canopy Way as it was sometimes called
made a magazine cover but it did not seem to influence any upswing of visitors
at all. The folks preferred this anyway. There was a report of a wily, clever
youth who was able to spend some of his time up in the canopy because of
his being light and very strong. The oaks could provide support but one
would have to be quite daring to try it. Reports were that he somehow
interwove securely some branches of the trees to each other in such a way as
to become a nest—like support for his probable also imagined adventures.
This was only partially suspected because a small plane pilot reported seeing
someone in the canopy but the pilot was accused of flying too low and he
had been drinking, so there was doubt about the report. The suspected youth

only shrugged when and smiled when questioned, so he left it open too. He was a school gymnast though. Many years ago the town made an agreement with the local city to sell its products, some of them well known, with the cites name on them and that also led to a certain anonymity to the town as well. This continued well for the folks and their families and even for the town. These were mostly special products grown on the towns two major farms, the other two quadrants taken up by the West End and the Neurological Complex's buildings and grounds. There was a lot of government funding for the Neurological Complex and the Director was a very astute man financially, and so there was good pay and plenty of work. Town celebrations and festivals for the most part had been canceled years ago as the people seldom attended. This was not out of disrespect or hostility, but more from the need to remain private with—so to speak—one's cards close to the chest. In a good way, this helped the town to save money and keep taxes very low. Rain in the town is important given the surrounding farms with crops. It also carries a mystical quality on Main Street because of the canopy. The rains more slide down than fall down. Thus it leads to a slowing of the wetting of the grounds looking jungle like. The gray of the day reflects the soul of the Town, a soul wearied by life and bittersweet moments of mild depression and despair. In a way, it brings the town folk closer in a slightly blue ochre manner. Another story going around the town involves the florist. She has been tied into, at least mentally as the housemistress in the West End of town although town folk believe that she can't make enough money at the shop most looked the other way.

Writer's Block . . .

The muse is gone again. No more pictures to tell, no more words to say, no more clicking in. Dried up and surprised about it but also not. Unsettled in my skin—something else going on and I don't know what it is. Some stirrings against my leavings and stream. An eroding of some kind that feels like stucco melting dryly away from its own skin. Bruises on the wall of the soul, inflicted by life's ups and downs. Too many roads to choose from, too many hearts to cry, too many dewdrops on windows and the rains pound to ask just why. Escaping through the pane goes the eyes of eiderdown flowing along a river walk through the valleys of the town. Mounted on a painted horse to screech the golden ring, falling back to sleep upon a regal queen or king. Enraptured by a rhythm sound and taken to the sky—to fly, to fly. Oh Hope, you futile promise and Fear you certain gain come together in a strident flash of pain. Give your often juices a rush through my veins pores till relief and joy come smashing through the bathroom backyard doors. Cats and dogs now truly smile at the persons for a while, gleeful in their mittens warm to run beneath the bee filled storm. Oh, please make sense of what I say I move through these thoughts with a day not filled with awaiting Death.

Writer's Block #2 . . .

Dry spells with occasional pouring through of information that he captures and holds like a butterfly till it gently lifts away. But now where are the words? Hidden under some deep rock that needs to be tumbled over. Are the words under there? Let's feel them and see if they can be used. Under the rock lies a golden sack filled with evergreen of the valley and love of the source. Reach into the sack for a discovery of joy perhaps a special word or phrase like 'a squint of a feeling' or 'blue . . . cool'. Is nothing stirring anew? Anxiety could be the block, performance anxiety, being seen, shamed—who wants to go there anymore? Maybe, perhaps, that may be where the words truly are at least the new ones that are formed by and are created by the end of the pen. It occurs between the borders of blue and hugs dropping line by line to the bottom of the page filling in above it with word new, archaic and satisfactory. Looking up the word can see only through where there are spaces and emotions that precede me and orient you as to how to take me with all of my possible meanings too. Most importantly if the muse does not kick in the writing will be dry, not fluid with alliterations and other English goodies. Flaunting along on a brace of support words eek out and through the tip of the pen. Sliding along above me is the line and between it and the notebook is me, a creative created word to be stored inside forever though I can be rained out like a ball game. Do the words come out of the pen? Where does the muse rest? In the mind, heart, hand, pen, or paper, or is it a whole of all of these being synchronized in time and space? How often do the words go across the boundaries—seldom unless you are an f or g or p and others with tails. Actually they are often hit from the words below as they hang down sometimes interfering on the next line's life. So words, sentences and phrases are very important and need to be treated with respect as they glide along unfolding the pages in one's mind and after giving others pleasure though not quite like the creator.

Fantasy & Dreams

Dream #1 . ✦ .

Slow moving turtle wings on grass of silver down
Sliding love in opaque jewels and sleeves
Coquetting along a hall in lovely French pink quills
Yellow cement blocking radical views
Maneuvering swells in sausage shells
Cooking leaves in barn stall hells
On the ground at last to sleep. Creep, creep, creep.

Fantasy #1 . . .

She looks at him with golden eyes, somewhat munching eyes. She can taste his ruggedness in her eyes. She smells his skin a combo baby man smell-so good. Her nose picks up on other scents of unions done so far. His taste lingers on her tongue satisfying and calling again. Her mouth, open slightly, mixing in the humid air into her lungs already expanded from love. He looks like a normal god like beauty. Can I really see him, picture him on the toilet-that'll ground him for me. No, don't go there, keep this magnificent! She touches him by leaning into him slowly so that the hair on his body yields rather than crunching in some intruded upon way. Her varying degrees of touch excite her smoothly. Some touches are light, some are strong. She presses into him where she thinks he lives-maybe a quarter inch below the surface. He let's out a sound, so she has reached him! She makes the same sound back to him hoping to mirror and engage in a sameness union of unending bliss. It will end but happen again in another male embrace. Beginnings and endings, being left drained and finding a new self there, is a repeating process. Each motion towards each other though supported by different affects each time, is trusted. (She much preferred the support of love in the movement). The sad motion, supported, led to easy crying, sorrowful sex, and relief. The angry motion, supported, led to lively, pumping sex and release of tension. The joy of motion, supported, led to fun, and laughter. She liked it however it happened. Right now she was enjoying the afterglow of this time—afterglow looks forward to the foreglow.

Fantasy #2 . . .

Sweet, so sweet she feels deep in her being. How did he know how to reach me in here. His touch, so delicate, so male, so firm, finds my heart and soul without even a word. Lying here nude with him is so precious, I want to indelibly mark this moment in my mind as I have so many others. The last time—always a prelude to the next time—has left me open and vulnerable to him here. Bodies touching with similar gestures performing their desired task. Melting into each other where do I end and begin? Where does he? I take his masculinity from him and I give my femininity to him so we are both a little less and a little more. My breasts give way to his harder front and it softens us and hardens us simultaneously unioning. His neck on mine—erotic and pulsing—makes us unite in another way. My eyes go limp and I take him in as he does me. My length covered by maleness reaches upward to the giver as I take. Boat movings gently swayed by waves of lasting love meets us fully. My face, maskless now, is a complete being as he is. Truth is emerging from profound places in us without argument in the meetings, near to overwhelm, I feel a movement-whole in my body—as the rushes begin to cascade down my soft mountainsides washing all away, and relieving and quiet unrumpled joy following after. Sailing into less difficult winds, I begin to come to myself recollecting my history and present. Yet I discover as if I had forgotten his presence—a boy teen man with me perspiring lovelets into me as close as close is. Don't move I feel, do not break this union spell. Entice me for the future now and I promise to be there too. Done, go.

The Wastebasket Series

The Wastebasket

How many have thrown into this basket? What has been thrown away? Ticket stubs, coffee cups and caps, register receipts, other crumpled paper and much more. The ticket stubs just before were carried in a shirt pocket alongside a pen and a post-it reminder. The man had just returned home alone and against his wishes. He had been with her and to dinner and a movie. A man's expectations again, weaker than a woman's wishes. Did he still have her ticket stub too? Well that is something anyway. She was pretty nice in a disorganized sort of way-somewhat sloppy but attractive too. What did he see in her? A certain motherly, girly, slutty, kind of female all wrapped up in one—a charmer of a sort. She was a baker at the store in town and part owner too. Her ex was the other owner. They must get along somehow well. Her specialty was Napoleons crème and crust and sugar. Her shop was well liked and respected by folks and on Sunday mornings, people flocked there for goodies. That is why he is with her tonight-Bakery closed on Monday. He kind of liked her quirky ways though he did not trust her as she was a bit flighty or flaky. He laughed! A bit short like Napoleon. He laughed again. Well I can enjoy myself about her. He had picked her up at her apartment and got a good look at it. Somewhat the way she dresses, a bit unkempt, not really tidy and a bit scattered. It surprisingly smelled wonderful to him, smells of his childhood home a sweet cookie muffin coffee kind. He felt relaxed there and warmhearted. She was kindly still as when at the bakery he asked her out. She's about 32 he guessed, never married he found out and hadn't dated much either. Reason? Loved her work—early to bed early to rise. Dinner was fine though she seemed a little on guard and he felt blocked and oriented by it, just a slight holding quality. He realized and knew from before a movie cuts out the connection though the ritualistic arm had an easy time. He might be with her now if he had gone to a café or dance place after dinner. What force dictates a couple to act in a patterned way? He did not know but the time felt patterned. Where had he heard that you can tell if a relationship will make it in the first 15 minutes? He felt this one wouldn't, but a little company . . .

Wastebasket #2
Register Receipts

$315.99 and $168.72 thrown into the wastebasket and just the last four numbers of the credit card show—no shredding necessary. She couldn't help it although she tried so hard. Spending, spending, spending. She was a shopaholic but did not call herself that. She was a professional woman and needed to look it and so having a lot of clothes was important. She had just decided to keep the items she had tried on at home again. Such decisions! Walking around the room checking all the angles in the mirror was part of the routine. Partially she admitted that she liked to strip her clothes off and then put something on. That's part of spending sprees-she gets to show herself off. She has a great figure—Madison Avenue type and she loved it. The only problem was the monthly monster she hated. She would try to hide it but it would come out of her against one of her boyfriends. She scared one of them intensely one time with her fierce, fiery feelings of anger and rage. She knew she held the rage of the ages of women insulted for centuries. He didn't call for a while but finally came around. He was her favorite sex partner but not her favorite boyfriend. Her favorite had a matching personality but not the bedroom prowess of this guy. How do married people do it with just one person? It requires giving up something but she was not ready to give up this yet. She loved sex long lasting and she loved men a lot. Some of her girlfriends did not like men and therefore sex too. Some denied it but she knew otherwise She was a doctor at the local hospital in town but she would have preferred being a streetwalker—she laughed—not really she thought . . .

Wastebasket #3, Hamptons . . .

Ann, please give me one more chance I love you so much, please don't throw it all away. Remember how we are in the best of times, remember the Hamptons, Seaside and Mt. Snow . . .

That was all there was. The rest of the letter was not in the wastebasket. Whose broken heart did we peek into? He had been dating her for three great years-yes she wanted marriage but he thought in time, in time . . . When she told him she wanted to date other men, his mind fell into a gaping hole that he did not know was there before. Struggling to gain control only to have his stomach be riddled with anxiety in response, he sat down before he would fall down. He did not want her to see him weakened and ready to throw up on his shirt front. He knew she always saw him as strong but not rite now. How did she get into him so deeply to have this kind of effect? Boy, was he crazy about her! What could she mean date others-a gentle let down? Aren't I all she wanted? I'm dizzy and sick and she looks like she is hanging from the ceiling like a marionette-what's happening to me!? Wait, I say to her, let's talk, she says fine with a balsamic vinegar tone that is new to me. What did I do wrong? How can that be? She only says she wants to see what else is out there to be sure of me-what a stupid fucking test this is!! Am I a possible dater? You know it can't be this way, you can't go backwards in a relationship, ninety nine percent of the time it fails. Now I am feeling a hot boiling rage inside me—what do I do with this?! And adding to the mix is my sexual arousal at the same time. She looks like a veil of a human and almost ghostlike as if I can see through her. I reach to her not even knowing I am choosing to and I say my date is the first and it is tonight! Her voice sounds like chalk on a blackboard now as she tells me to leave her alone in fact—leave now! Something happens to me in this emotional mess that explodes me into a raging humanless, animal figure passionate about life and death. Death is drawing me nearer and I take her by the throat and begin to strangle her while almost watching from afar. She weakly struggles but I am a monstrous animal, pure red and black, and destructive, and I kill her, kill her, kill her, with my mind, body and soul-but I would never do such a thing!! I am an accountant for a respectful firm in town. I would never do such a thing. This isn't really happening. Only the people in the neurological complex in town would do this kind of act. Yet, here in front of my eyes it is happening I am making life leave this body like I am a God or something. But I love her and want her alive not dead as she dies in my now deviled arms. Don't die!! I can give death and I can give you life! Now, take life back I did not mean this! But she does not take life back. Why won't she take this gift?. A human being died last night . . .

Later, after my confinement, I realize that it was a little—not-also more than a crime of passion. I am also a bit nutty too. My punishment is to be in this complex and be the healthiest and actually see what ongoing crazy means. Mine was just temporary insanity, I think. That Dr. Joe is in here and he is mostly in his room rocking or sitting there being a crazy man. I went to him only one time cause there was something strange about him his eyes were too blank for me and it feel eerie . . .

Wastebasket #4, Coffee Cups . . .

Crumpled coffee cups and a mix of other things in the wastebasket. Ruby red lipstick edging one border. A kissed up or merely drinking? The women's lips had left a mighty impression on the cup much like the impression she had left on her boyfriend's member. She loved him very much and wanted to please him. She liked her lipstick marks on him sought of like dropping blood dried in place. Don't we always have something red at all meals? At this meal her red lips filled the bill and he filled her mouth with his errant sons and daughters who would not be. They had just finished the coffee and thru them into the wastebasket. Conversationally both were adequate, but being ok with silence, they had a lovely way about them. In silence he would put his right hand fingers on her clitoris and his left hand into her vagina at the G spot and rock her back and forth into a combustible bliss and drenching. She didn't know where she went but knew nothing but animal feelings—no mind, no soul. Please don't stop she begged early on and now he would go on until she almost bled thru her pores—a sweet blood—it would be drinkable, edible, and satisfying. Blood that would rush into her soul and heart and restore her. Her sweat came along as well, hot sweaty salty, wet. She would see him lick her up as if he had found some olden nectar of the goddesses from which he could feed and drink. He was patient, slow, and thorough and after each session he would spank her into pain. The first time she was scared but then opened to the sadomasochism of it all and looked forwards to and relished the beatings. She knew and felt aliveness like at no other time. She vibrated with brittle body and breath. She loved him very much. At the coffee bar they looked like regular people and in fact they were to all appearances. She wondered on occasion if he wanted a gay experience as he always wanted her dildo up his behind or her fingers on his prostate driving him 120 miles an hour into the fiercest orgasms, which left him so spent, she thought he had passed out. They loved to make love with passion, roughness and tenderness too. But this day, this coffee morning day, was a special day as he proposed to her in the coffee shop while eating a chocolate frosted donut but both she and he knew it came from the heart.

Wastebasket #5, Second Son . . .

A paperback entitled," The Second Son." To whom did this belong? After a cursory look at the novel, I get that it is about the second Son of God. The reader must have been a semi-religious man. He had once been an altar boy when mass was still said in Latin. He never fully understood the language but he loved the rituals and mystery of it all. He became a frequent churchgoer, in fact, very dedicated with thoughts of becoming a priest. When he became sexually aware, he was influenced in a different way. The hot, intense, driving impulse in masturbation consumed him daily. What a wonderful feeling, and girls looked different, attractive. His mind was full of women walking naked and calling him time and again. The fight, anguish, and torture of the adolescent years had begun. Saint/Sinner, Madonna/Whore, Good/Bad, Right/Wrong, the crippling conflicts over and over again unceaseingly continued to this just a boy. Guilt and shame believed deeply and felt as well, a thorough machination and manipulation by the church. So, body and mind at war, each winning omnipresent battles. God and the Devil, Lucifer and Jesus fight in him to this day. He often thought of himself as the second son but now he knew otherwise. The conflict was still there but it had lessened a good deal, as he is 56 years old.

Wastebasket #6 . . .

A cell phone? Is it still useable? How did it get there? Any numbers left on it? A technology burial ground of some kind. The owner was a young man in his thirties who had used it for many drug deals but was now trying to go straight. This tossing of the phone was his first act to begin to remove himself from this world he lived in so long a time. Avoiding places he frequented, people he knew and had hung out with for years, was going to be difficult. He had lived the life so long and all that came with it for him. As he became a dealer he had most of it for free and that included the girls. The girls would think nothing of having sex with anyone and hopping out of bed with a laugh and leave the room as if nothing had happened—no meaning at all. Now they would not be able to call him for drugs, sex, and rock and roll. This, his first day, in his first attempt to go straight was very difficult as he knew only those on drugs and missed them. Where can I go now for the day and what about when nighttime comes? Sitting here in this diner I am like a rocking schizophrenic. This can be the withdrawal and I may not make it. It feels like there is a hand in my head squeezing at random my brains. This rocking is not comforting and it is drawing eyes toward me, fuck 'em! God damn it! My skin feels like it is crawling up and down my body like a window shade. Am I actually feeling the insides of my teeth? My heart is pounding, I need a 'fix' I hear in my brain but I also hear no not this time. I am happy about that and panic stricken at the same time. My craving and longing are on fire, How can I or why should I say no? One day at a time. I need more coffee and a cigarette just to see the next moment. This longing reminds me of my longing for my father, a distant, lonely man. He was yearning for his dad probably. Well, men with their addictions, close buddies who satisfy their longings. These buddies' shut them down sexually in reality, and in fantasy. They bed down with them in intimacy and depth of feeling. The addiction says, "I am your friend for life."

Wastebasket #8, Vick's VapoRub

Vick's VapoRub!? What the hell is the matter with you!? My anger spewed forth from me. How could she defy me so openly? I could smash her one and I almost did. My baby doctor said, "None of that stuff." I fired her on the spot. Eating my goddamned food and using my toilet, too Bitch! These fucking foreigners are all over the place now. My doctor did warn me against hiring her but she was all I could find. He said he thought she did serve time at the complex in town but the records from then were sealed. If I had had time to investigate her, I would know she had come from Puerto Rico and she was suspected of criminal behavior although never arrested or prosecuted. Some babies she had taken care of had mysteriously died and one had completely disappeared. Unknown to all of us is that she was a cannibal and in fact had eaten a baby totally to the bone—flesh, muscles, fat and sinew—all of it. She ate some of the baby with jalapeño jelly—her favorite. She used Vicks as a distraction, making all the mothers and fathers become olfactory aware. This became their obsession and their vision became less due to this diverted intention. This scheme allowed for the Puerto Rican to use her eyes to an advantage over the mothers. She would think, "Although I cannot have a baby vaginally, I can have one orally." She had only eaten three babies in total and she had to have wine before she did it. White wine, she chuckled. She remembered looking in the mirror and seeing baby blood on her jaw and chin. It startled her for a moment as she thought of it. How weird am I!! She chastised herself. Well anyway, here I am fired again. I should leave this town anyway—a bunch of locos and pendejos

Wastebasket #9, Lipstick Tube . . .

That sound its driving me crazy everywhere I go-computers. Cast off as the wrong color, she continued on down the street. The color reminded of the lion she saw in her dreams last night. Why the lion? She really wasn't an aggressive woman although she remembers some times when she was and had to be. What about the anaconda? Someone was brining it straight to her face this is the one thing she feared more than anything. She had created a snake in a box tied to her head with the only way out was though her face., It frightened her so much. She put together, after some thought, a sexual aggression. She had not had sex in a while and was ok about it but her unconscious may be telling her otherwise. The lipstick the color of the lion in her dream looked awful on her. The skin was not a good match at all. Now what about that penis anaconda? No association came to her. Why are all these people trying to kill her in her dreams/nightmares? The doctors said it was the meds but she only half believed them. She was nearly killed by knives, guns animals and people. What are they trying to kill? A guilty part of me? An angry part of me? She wished she knew. If it was guilt why just the torturer and not completion of the act? Guilty say I am guilty, torture says I known I will make you pay in your sleep at night. Guilt says I fear you not knowing when you are coming nor what nor how you'll do you or be you. Torture says I am your surprise I am your spontaneity I am your cleverness and your energy. Guilt says I do not fear you once I awake and you are seeing me less and less although I still react with intensity. I think it is physiological more than anything. Torture says well I will try harder. Integration interrupts and says what would d be the offspring of a union between Guilt and torture? Torturer is perp and guilt is victim Guilt says I do not want to be victim. Torture says I am ambivalent about being a perpetrator. Sadomasochism? Another way to look. How to break free. Through a new agreeing and negotionable to a new resolution.

She knew nothing about these dynamics but hoped telling them out might make her nights a little less crazy. As she went along thinking she suddenly bumped into someone who was big and fast at grabbing her shoulders before she went down. Pissed off she told the guy to watch where he was going and he said the same to her. My he is a swarthy and some thing she thought while rearranging herself. He eased into a smile, one of welcome. She began to smile back and he said, after crashing into you perhaps a cup of coffee would refuel you for a while on your walk. She said yes and walked off with him.

Wastebasket #10, An Herbal Essence . . .

"Oh, I didn't know," her English, Singaporean accent exclaimed. He thought how could she think that after inviting him into her room at two o'clock in the morning. He had asked at her doorway as they were parting after the evening show. "Do you want to get together?" "Yes," she said. What could be more of an invite to her statement? Once inside the small room she asked him if his bed were bigger or longer than hers. He heard that she wanted more room than was on this bed. She pointed to him to sit in the only although uncomfortable chair. He agreed. After some time of conversing superficial topics, he looked at her and said, "Do you want to lie down?" A startled "no" bounced off her lips and onto his ears. "Did you think when I said yes that sex was what I was saying yes to when we came into my room? It was just to chat." Crestfallen, he looked away. How could he be so wrong? She asked," What did I do that suggested I wanted to do it??" He said that he thought she was saying yes by letting him come into her bedroom and at two in the morning She was surprised that he didn't think that the invite was just to chat. "I am a late night person, I stay up until three every morning so, I didn't think anything of it to ask you in to chat. After being reminded of her comment about bed size she said, "I did not know" again in that silky English seaside tone. A bit frustrated he said, "What about if you just show me your body?" Again, English lilt laughter lightly leans into his question. "She said I am not laughing at you and I won't undress for you and if you keep on this line of thinking you will have to leave." Taking a 'no' is not easy but this time it was given without rejection and so landed very smoothly and sweetly onto an open runway ear. "I m embarrassed a little." She said. "Don't be because I am also flattered by it." Internally he wondered what that might mean but decided to leave it alone. What is she putting into her hands that she now offers to me? Some kind of incense smell that you first put on your hands then rub them together and then place them like a cup over your nose and gently breathe in. Intoxicating, like her. Perhaps she unknowingly wants me to take her smell with me but nothing else. She throws it into the wastebasket. I think maybe it is some drug inducing aphrodisiac. I am projecting again. Got to go to my own room and sleep. At least she cannot say no inside my mind.

The Spiritual

A Walk in the Evening . . .

Amber alleyways toning the sidewalks with hued shades
Neon counterbalancing the natural earth given tones
Fancy shapes forming receptacles of warmth in the glowing night
Streetside flowers flowing down the lanes
Cupcake bows in pots and boxes along the old storefronts
Walking people in relaxed, soulful joy strides in peace

A Bead Store . . .

Beads of many colors
Of glasses and jewels and earth
Prices from ground to skyrocket
To fit each and every pocket
From all over the world
Come these tiny blessings
Giving peace and creativity
To all who meet them

Divine Light . . .

Divine Light and Holy Spirit dissolve this problem now. Even cellular memories can be released from deep within. All the repressed originally for safety sake dissolve now. Come to the surface let me feel them and show me what they want. All ancestral energies from the blight and famine be released now. Endocrine system, nervous system, belief system, value system emotional and all physical systems be released, felt, known and healed now! Layer upon layer, deeper and deeper, reveal my divine presence to me! Divine Spirit infuse me with your love and joy and laughter. Release me from all dark sources and heal them too with your Divine light. Oh Dear Lord Jesus move my heart in compassionate, empathic and loving ways. Let me be receptive to your guidance and care and presence. Heal my sinning ways so entangled in darkness to be lost. Free me to the light of glory and blessings from You, your Father, and Spirit.

Lord Jesus . . .

Dear Lord Jesus, friend in my background, healer through me. Please stay with me for a time in a way I know your presence. I need you and now more than ever. I am weakening and I need to find strength in some ways to cope with what I will have to deal with. I know this is me, me, me, but to whom else can I turn in the spiritual world but you and your father and the Spirit. Overwhelm me with an infusion of Divine Grace. Make me be a sacred healer because of this challenge. "Oh Lord I am not worthy that I should come under thy roof." Yet you are under mine which makes me worthy. You are the footprints in the sand and I am on your back. Please carry me all the way home. Cleanse me of my doubt, let me see you soon again. Wink an eye, or raise an arm or some other gentle sign. Keep my progression slow as I want to do more work and attempt to heal more. Create more visibility for those who cannot see. Help me to get writing again too. Help me pass through blocks I may encounter on my way. Let my character come alive in town and interact together in a good way.

Miracle at Cana . . .

What a nice wedding but it sure is hot here in the desert. Thanks that my sandals are broken in cause the ground and heat at my feet would be too much. The couple look good in their roges of different colors. The whole town is here I think and it is my guess that they will run out of wine soon as I can tell there is definitely not enough. We'll all switch to water here in the hot wedding sun. There are so many people here including the town drunks who probably are the ones who will drink it all up fast. I was invited to the wedding as I am the second cousin of the bride. I don't particularly like the husband—too smug, arrogant, or know what allish. He didn't come from Cana, which is not bad, but could cause disagreements in child-rearing practices as the neighboring town of Arimethea tends to be very strict with their kids. Well just as I predicted, the wine has run out. There is some guy about two groups away from me saying to bring him the water and he will turn it into wine. Boy these people who think they are like God or better! It will take a miracle to do what he is saying. He probably is some voodoo witchcraft kind of person anyway. It is happening I can't believe it but the glass that just was poured for me was wine and I know for sure there was no more wine. This guy is amazing! They're calling Him, Jesus, a miracle worker. I moved to get into a closer position to Him while making sure I did not spill my wine. He is just sitting and labeling out water that turns into wine in the glass. I want to know how to do this! I dump my wine behind the rock. I want to get more and get closer to Him. Now just a few feet away, I notice a slight smell of flowers but I don't see them around anywhere. I begin to feel the arthritis in my hip acting up. I extend my glass and say, "Thank you." He looks into my eyes, not at me. What a powerful experience. My pain disappeared and I stood nice and tall for the first time in quite a few years. I want to tell Him but someone had his attention. I have heard there are healers around that can do this kind of thing but the wine one is a little hard to explain. At the first of opportunity I say to him, "what are you doing to the water?" He says, "Pouring into wine glasses not water glasses." I smiled, a knowing one as he also smiled a friendly smile and I said to him, "You are a healer". He said, "Yes. I Am." The wine started to get to me so I wandered off to say my good lucks to the Bride and Groom. Next, I headed home as I wanted to tell my family about the strange events of the day-strange—as they were to me, and the others.

Morning thoughts . . .

Oh God, let me use today as a beginning to walk in the greatness of Your Son Jesus. Let me follow his path, an honest, authentic, alive path meeting the good, the bad and the ill along the way, yet seeing the promise in each of their hearts. Give me the gift of vision to see this way. Make my eyes be a source for your presence. Help me to see the beauty in all and everyone. As the day opens to the morning sun and sounds, let me touch the deepest part of myself in new ways led by your plantings on my path. Let me see thru the dark alcoholic pain, the deceptive one's pain, the cheater and liar and thief's pain. Let me see their true nature though now occluded by terror. I pray that they see thru the darkness and into a brighter place. Let me rid myself of all sins especially of gluttony and vaingloriuosness and all my other ones and then I can claim to be fully one of yours. Let not my hypocrisy or self-importance be the block to being with you. Make me tender and warm. Help me to care more for the children and alienated ones around us, for in many ways, I am like them too. Lift me out of my sometimes despair so that I might use what I have for the best that I can. Let me be a faithful companion along the way and a faithful servant for you. Let it all make sense and be good in your eyes and not be sanctioned and subjugated by man.

Some God thoughts . . .

Contemplative heart of Jesus reach into my soul with the love that is in You and render me whole. Deep intimacy with God is my inspiration, please allow it to fill without false elation. Let my truth be felt, told and only mine from which I am inured. Oh God, please help me in this time of alienation. Bring me strong back to your glorious nation, humble me with love and divine presence. Show me you in all your simplicity here now in everything I see. You exist in all not in pantheism but in truthful glory and outburstness. Like an acorn to an oak I start at the beginning of it all. Help me, help me, help me.

Printed in the United States
135788LV00002B/11/P

9 781436 335768